Opportunities in Alabama Agriculture

by

Tito Perdue

Books by Tito Perdue

Lee (1991)
The New Austerities (1994)
Opportunities in Alabama Agriculture (1994)
The Sweet-Scented Manuscript (2004)
Fields of Asphodel (first ed., 2007; second ed., 2023)
The Node (2011)
Morning Crafts (2013)
Reuben (first ed., 2014; second ed., 2022)
The Builder: William's House I (2016)
The Churl: William's House II (2016)
The Engineer: William's House III (2016)
The Bachelor: William's House IV (2016)
Cynosura (2017)
Philip (2017)
Though We Be Dead, Yet Our Day Will Come (2018)
The Bent Pyramid (2018)
The Philatelist (2018)
The Smut Book (2018)
The Gizmo (2019)
Love Song of the Australopiths (2020)
Materials for All Future Historians (2020)
Journey to a Location (2021)
Vade Mecum (2021)

Opportunities in Alabama Agriculture

by

Tito Perdue

Standard American Publishing Company-
Brent, Alabama
2023

Cover image:
Anne Goldthwaite, *Cabin in Alabama* (c. 1915–1925)
Smithsonian American Art Museum

Cover design by Kevin Slaughter

Hardcover ISBN: 978-1-64264-031-1
Paperback ISBN: 978-1-64264-032-8

Contents

Prologue

Followed then six years in silence. For if it were otherwise in old times, now it had come to this, that he dwelled on nine acres near to the edge of the world. Have I said he had ten brothers? Each more ignorant than the other? Himself most ignorant of all? Sin too, sin was there, so much of sin that all had taken to keeping their faces covered, yea all day, yea, even in their many tasks. And if once Wade did rush from the opening, his face girded-up in self-punishment, yet soon the sun would drive him back.

Moaning in the cabin. He had given anything, all and everything, if only it were further along in the history of the world.

Moaning in the light. It was all sin, all, and a new volcano that had come up during the night, pushing the cabin higher. Ignorant altogether, he loved to go running in it, down to where the acres ended, there to sit with his feet dangling over the side and with the head of his tamed lizard resting in his lap.

First, the sky was red. Everywhere, the new-made stars were dispersing to their separate corners. And once he almost screamed out loud, owing to a certain blue planet that seemed aiming straight for him.

There was much he did not understand; it was late, the moon was down, he saw three brothers racing for the cabin. And when the sun did come, and he fainted, the first farmer witnessing the first dawn, he fainted. Years passed, or days. Or perhaps he slept.

And now the day was high.

One

At that period, when the colors of things were as yet indeterminate, and the various tints were prone to running all over the page upon which those same tints were mentioned, at that time Time itself afflicted him severely. Already, the cabin had burnt. Mule too—badly scorched. Ben did, however, still spy him from time to time, still breathing, still a mule. Suddenly, his face covered, Wade dashed from the cabin and stumbled out into the field where he lay, groaning at the sun.

"Nine" acres, I said? Those days, when he went down to the Edge, in fact the distance was further, owing to the number of cow chips that the old man had pasted there one by one. Therefore in great pride, it was eleven acres now, no longer just nine. And then too, eleven made a better showing among the planets.

Moaning in the cabin, one of the brothers had died. Never was Ben to forget it, when at last they lifted off the cloth that had for so long covered his face. That night, with moaning in the cabin, he crawled along the floor, checking the face of each surviving brother. To his father, he did *not* crawl. His father had the bed, and did his moaning several inches off the floor.

Year after year, and still the Time would never stop, never turn, never go back to whence it had come. But mostly it was the deteriorating sun itself; was he the only one to see that it had begun to flicker out?

It was a good day, that when the first planted agricultural row crops began to make an appearance in the acres that were not yet dark. He spent long days, coordinating the growths with stick, glove, and scissors. (He had learned to get quickly out of the way for each new volcano that came up.) But his father, who went abroad without his face-covering, his father nowadays spent the better part of his days scaling up and down the "sun-tower" fabricated from disused wasp nests, his memorial to his wife. They passed without speaking.

It was in his fifteenth year, the colors still running, when a bee came and, saying nothing, bit him on his scissor's finger. Ben groaned, suffering from the knowledge of the coming of the insects to his twenty-acre world. And when he looked up, it was not just clouds he saw; groaning, he saw (and heard) the braying mule tumbling slowly in orbit.

Winter came and passed, and although he sat out the whole time among his agricultural row crops, yet the crops did poorly. Spring he dreaded, knowing now about the insects and the reeking world.

So the days. Slowly and slowly, the colors did congeal upon the page. Very seldom now did he go all the miles down to the Edge—it was further, the stars more settled. He believed the world had thirty acres to it, believed it steadfastly, even up until that morning he heard a rooster crowing on other acres that belonged to someone else.

Two

In 1883, Ben crossed the road. He was older now, the world larger, and for a long time he had been wishing to visit the next farm. "And just how many farms might there not be?" he wondered, getting no answer. Suddenly, he stopped and gathered up a nodule of glass out of the red clay roadbed. Very few such reminders were still left over from the volcano age; nevertheless, he tossed it away indifferently into the trees. The day itself was clear, the sky putting on a slightly different aspect each time he looked. Behind him were hills, smoke coming off the summits, and in the bottoms four burnt cabins forming a row in front of his mother's tomb. He was about to continue on when, just then, the old man stumbled out into view and, scowling furiously, began to shake his stick in a threatening manner at the sun. As for his brothers, those that survived, he saw one here and one there, and saw Willard sleeping betimes in the open.

Ben trudged on. In those days, the highway was already very old, old and worn and covered in an inch of bright red powder that lapped about the toes. There was much he did not understand—the weather and the day, the crows that gathered from all corners to jeer him on his way. If whistling, this was the time to fall silent, and if talking to himself, now he began to speak too noiselessly to be overheard.

The road bent northward, carrying him out of view of the cabin and of his own people. The last he wanted now was for a wagon to come along and to offer him a ride that he could not well refuse. For it was only when he was alone and out of view of the cabin, only then that he could talk to himself in the way that he wished. And then too, he expected to remember this day, which promised to be both the best that he had ever had, and therefore better by far than any that might follow thereafter. Slowly, refusing to look at it, he passed the "settlement"—four ruined homes abandoned before he had been born and now entangled in vines. Nor would he think about it, nor look at it, not today, nor dwell upon it in his mind. On the contrary! he moved past in dignity, glancing neither to the gate nor tower, nor to the one remaining window pane where a certain dear face—he had heard the stories—might be waiting still. Instead, he took up a stone, an ore with red veins in it, and threw in where the crows were thickest. It was when he looked behind him that he saw how his own excursion had left a more childish course (dashing here and there) than he would have

thought of himself. That was when the lizard came lop-
ing up, miffed at having been left behind.

They approached slowly, hesitating to set down foot
upon someone else's land. A woman, (and Ben had heard
all about her), a woman was sitting in the swing shelling
peas. A minute went by, the two of them looking at each
other steadily across the space. Now she lifted one enormous hand, shielding her eyes in order to take a nearer
look.

"Vernon's boy?"

"Yes, ma'am."

"Well, come on up here then. Lands! That old tree
ain't going to fall over, you don't have to hold it up. So
Vern's done gone and died then."

"Ma'am?"

"Not dead?"

"No, ma'am."

"Well why do you want to be over here then?"

"Visit." (He saw her hand drop, and then saw it stir-
ring about in the peas.) "I brung a present."

"My, my. Garbert! we got a visitor. He can't hear,
chopping down in them woods. Now what could it be, I
wonder, in that there little bag? You didn't go and put no
snake in there, did you?"

"No, ma'am! It's persimmons."

"Persimmons! My, my. We got lots of them."

He watched her take the bag and then place it down
delicately next to her in the swing. That she must certainly have children, he had divined it from the quantity
of peas that she had shelled.

"Y'all got any little boys over here?"

"Yes sir, ole Vern's dead for sure—*that's* what ran
through my mind. When I seen you slinking up here."

"Yes, ma'am. No, ma'am; he's not dead."

"Working on his 'altar'?"

"Yes, ma'am."

"Hee! I'm just surprised you boys ain't starved by now. Virgil still got that 'woman' living over there?"

"No, ma'am. She left."

"Well."

"Frank left too."

"I'm real happy to hear that. Garbert! He can't hear. I swear, he's been down in those woods *all morning*."

"Yes, ma'am. Your children, I reckon they're down in them woods too, I reckon."

"No. No, they're up here somewhere. Bound to be. You seen 'em?"

"No, ma'am. How many you got?"

"Well, there's Thymus. That's one. But you don't want *him*."

"No, ma'am."

"*You* want Belinda."

Ben said nothing. From the sound of it, he was not so sure it was what he wanted.

"And Lucerne, there's *her*."

"Yes, ma'am."

"Well? That's two right there. How many do you got to have?"

"Just two."

"Well alright. 'Course now, Lu's been sick."

"Yes, ma'am."

They looked at each other.

"Well? You want 'em, or not?"

"Yes, ma'am."

"Well go find 'em then! Lands! I swear, when it comes to *doing* things . . ."

He leapt down from the porch. At the side of the house, some thirty chickens were at once thrown into dismay at his appearance, and that of his pet. Came next the windmill, the tallest feature within five miles. He was looking up at it when he realized the woman was watching from around the corner.

"Them girls ain't up there."

"No, ma'am."

The orchard proved full of cows; looking more closely, he saw also where a goat had gotten mixed up with the herd. With a farm like this one, heavy with apples . . . He was not so certain he belonged in the same county with such people.

The two girls were in front of the barn; Ben marched up straightway to the tall one and then, spitting on the ground, looked off afar into the dead volcanos that formed a congestion on the eastern horizon. His mental processes, of course, told him that the shorter girl, the one left over, could only be the other one. Both girls were in dresses that came down to the ground, both holding giant wooden hammers of some kind.

"Pshaw," said Ben.

"Who are you!"

"And what are you doing with them 'hammers,' that's what I'd like to know."

"Who are you!"

"I live over yonder. Most times." He pointed. "I'm Vernon's boy, one of 'em."

Belinda went pale. Lucerne backed away.

"Naw, I ain't going to hurt you."

"Well I reckon not! This is *our* farm."

"I know that! I just come over here to *visit*."

"And that's our house."

They turned and looked at it.

"I know it's your house! Did I say it wern't?"

"And that's our daddy too."

In fact, the man had come from the woods, had stopped, and now was grinning at them across the field.

"I know it's your daddy!" (He looked for something that was *his*.)

"Yes, and I reckon he can take care of *you* most any time he wants to."

"I know that! And Frank can take care of *him*."

Lucerne blenched. He knew so little about women. And yet, he felt absolutely certain that if need came to it, he could have thrashed both of them together at the same time.

"And what are them 'hammers' for?"

They giggled, a sound that was not familiar to him. That Belinda was "pretty," he was as confident of that as that he could have thrashed her, should the need prove necessary.

"They're not 'hammers.' Lands! They're 'mallets.'"

"Oh Lord. I know that!"

"We were *trying* to play croquet. Before *you* come along."

Ben shrugged and looked off across the draw where— and this did surprise him—they had peach trees too. As to "croquet," he hadn't the smallest idea of what they were talking of. He was thinking seriously of turning and going back home; instead, with both girls following closely, he stepped into the barn and looked about in it with boredom and disappointment. He knew about barns; he did *not* know about barns with separate chambers for each several cow.

"Well come on in," he said, "if you're coming. They got some cotton in here."

"We know."

The stuff indeed was high, deep, lush, and clean; right away, he clambered to the top and then, with the girls watching, allowed himself to go rolling downhill in it, till he hit the floor. It was easy; his plan was to do it again and again, until they understood that fear meant nothing whatsoever to him, and never would. Belinda wanted to do it too.

"Now don't blame me if you get kilt," he said. "I warned you."

In fact, she did very well, and came out laughing. A

game like this, it was the reason he had wanted to go visiting in the first place. And if already he was addicted to the sound of girls screaming, now he need only to order them into the basket, throw the cat in with them, and then shove the whole mess downhill.

"Fun, ain't it?"

They admitted it.

"See? You could have been doing this a long time ago. If you'd *thought* about it." Then: "I got to pee now."

They waited. Hurriedly, he ran around to the rear where—and this had always been his grandmother's saying—where he could be seen only by the black-eyed peas, and heard only by the ears of corn. He was by no means finished with the cotton and yet, when he got back, Lucerne had taken a jar of molasses from somewhere and was struggling to get it open.

"Oh Lord!" said Ben. "Here, let *me* do it, *I* can do it."

He was not accustomed to this willingness to let him do things, and yet he liked it however. He had his way and the whole world would be full of such people. Nor did the bottle give him much trouble; he was able to pry off the lid while still wearing a bored expression.

"Take it, take it, take it."

Lucerne reached for it and drank. No one had wanted her to consume *all* of it.

"Hey!" He took it back and gave it to Belinda who, however, realized that it was him who had opened it, and him who had invented the fun in the cotton. She gave it back.

"It's good!" said Ben. "*Pretty* good."

Belinda drank, doing it more courteously than her sister. All around was silence, and the sun finding glints of gold deep within the fluid. He would remember the moment, he did not know why.

"It's good!" she said. "A little bit."

"Want more?"

"No! Do you?"

"Not me! Lu does."

They stood by. She was good at it, Lu, and soon enough the sun was striking, not golden molasses, but the blue-and-grey-tinted jar itself, altogether empty.

"Gracious!" said Belinda. "See what I mean about her? That's just the way she is! Every day!"

They went on. The gander, a determined-looking personality, had gotten into the geese, but then had turned and come running out in wild alarm. In the distance, Ben now spotted the three dogs, William, Henry, and Edward, all of them gazing out languidly from under the house. He now had a girl on his left and a girl on his right, both with tads of cotton adhering in their hair. He knew nothing about the hair of girls, save that it was long, brown, and had tads of cotton in it. But all that was as nothing when compared to the innocent spot, a tiny little void, behind Belinda's ear; he could not take his eyes off that place. That was when a strange thought occurred to him, namely that if ever anyone should try to *beat* her, instead he would himself beat that person.

They moved on. One of the girls was humming but, for the life of him, he could not discern which one. The sun now was high, sky blue, and the clouds, (on this his happiest of all days), had not budged in several hours. As to the cows, they were of various colors, each of them facing off in the direction of his, or her, own choosing. He had few cows in the place where he came from. Lucerne, however, treated them with contempt.

"Shoo! Dumb old thing. Git!"

Ben too, he began to shoo at them as well, until he noted another animal, *not* a cow, who was feeding in the same field with them—a black-and-white goat, well-bearded, with milky eyes.

"Be careful!" said Belinda. "He don't like boys."

"Shoot. Well maybe *I* . . ."

He had started to say: "Well maybe *I* don't like *him*." Instead, that moment, the animal charged straight toward him. He simply could not believe this was happening, not on the part of a goat whom he had never wronged in any way whatsoever. He had just time enough to take a last lingering look at the sky and its constellations. It was not death he feared, but to be seen lying in a cow pat, seen by girls. Both came running.

"That blamed old Chester! I hate him!"

"I hate him too," said Ben.

"Well, at least you didn't get any doo on you." She looked for damage. The goat had gone off some distance where he stood grinning and chewing and, apparently, reflecting on whether to attack again. Ben moved with dignity to the nearest tree, climbing quickly and with skill, almost to the top of it. From here, he could see much—the bin and barn, the cattle and pond, and the long green sward of pasture that lapped the highway. He saw his father's tower, and further, saw smoke lifting from a certain hill that in due course might someday erupt again. He experienced great sadness, knowing that this, the best day he would ever know, knowing it was half over already and wasting fast.

Belinda had taken the next tree and was swaying slightly in the breeze. They were good climbing girls, these; in *her* tree, Lucerne was scanning far. And then Ben saw what he assumed to be the tiny Thymus, a soiled boy in pants and suspenders who had taken up a quarter of a mile away in the tallest tree of all. They all looked at one another, all of them swaying in measure. However— and nothing was ever *absolutely* perfect—Belinda soon came down again. *Her* tree had spiders in it.

Ben came down too, bringing two apples with him. Belinda was on her knees, drinking out of both hands from the creek. He saw the spot behind her ear, gazing upon it in a kind of horror. Again, a general silence seemed to have afflicted the farm and field, save only for the noise of an insinuating fly who visited each of them in turn. Once more, against his will and his best interest, he was again storing up photographs in his head, the first time he had done so since the Edge of the world. Just now, the girl had come down close to the surface of the water and was watching a tiny brown crayfish trundling across the floor of the creek. In this county, there were two such species, one of them brown and the other gold. *This* one, however, wore the heaviest armor that Ben had ever yet seen.

"He's drinking," said Lu.

"No, he's having dreams."

"No, combing his hair."

"Oh! 'Hair.' Sometimes I worry about you, Blinda."

"Hey! There's his wife."

"That ain't no wife! Besides, she's all brown."

"Oh."

"Girls are yellow."

That was true.

"They know you're looking at them. It's not nice."

"You're looking too!"

That was true. Blinda was the first to roll over and leave the things in peace. The grass *was* lush; he found himself looking up into a sky in which, so it seemed to him, a thin pale vapor was running behind the sun. There was something in this day. And when he looked at Belinda, there was something *there* too. But he didn't know what it was.

"Hey! Don't be looking at me. Gracious."

"How come?"

"'Cause! We have to sleep now."

Indeed, Lucerne, who had gone off a distance, looked to be asleep already. In the place where he came from, there was only one of his brothers who slept in the day-time, and out-of-doors. And yet . . . The grass *was* deep, the day warm, and Chester far away.

Many other things happened on that day. Later on, he was to remember only that they had withdrawn into the house itself, the evening having come down on them more rapidly than he would have thought possible. (Years still must pass before the days would have any sort of resemblance, one to another, in length or clarity.) Ten minutes went by while he sat in silence, abashed by the great height of the rooms that went from floor to ceiling. Abashed too that Belinda sat next to him on the couch, thumbing through her photograph album. Across from them sat the small Thymus, a mean-looking quantity, soiled and wearing no shirt.

"There they are!" Belinda said, pointing to the page. "John, James, and Zebulon."

Ben looked closer. James seemed to be a mule. Some of these photographs reached back into times when a milky fog had suffused the world. One picture was so engulfed with it that the people (if any there were) would have needed to communicate by touch alone. He saw next a bearded man, an old one, and in a photograph that was itself ancient. The person stood in what appeared to be a newly-harrowed field, smiling back evilly from beyond the tomb.

"Who's *that* one!"

"We don't know. Sarah used to know."

"Sarah?"

"She's dead."

Just then, Ben glanced up to find Belinda's father, a shy man, smiling in the door. They nodded briefly, and then the farmer blushed and moved away. That was when Belinda bent and whispered excitedly: "We're having ice cream tonight!" He saw her hand on the album, and saw how the nails were chewed down to nothing, the result of the non-stop excitement in a household like this one. Ben said nothing. Outside, the crickets were putting up a tremendous noise, until they all suddenly stopped at the same instant in order to give the tree frog his chance. Now came Lucerne, who had put on lipstick and a sweet-smelling lotion of some kind. She sat on his left-hand side. He was quite happy; he could not, however, move. The farmer himself had gone off into the next room where he sat smoking in the dark.

Ben had promised not to let himself be intimidated by anything. And yet the table, and the food upon it, this intimidated him greatly. Almost the first thing he noticed was a little brown pot of honey in which one of the original bees had drowned. He saw no ice cream anywhere, not yet. There *was* sweet-potato pie—he could definitely see how the potatoes themselves were nudging for space within the syrup. Too courteous to break the crust, he waited for someone else to do it. Instead, he reached for the biscuits, but then quickly drew back in again when he saw that the people were saying prayers. There followed a long silence. Then:

"Let Benjamin have a biscuit, Blinda. Seems he just can't wait."

"Put some of that green jelly on it, Ben!" said the farmer, who then blushed and fell silent. "If you want to, I mean."

Indeed there were jellies of several sort, each laid out in a delicate dish with an accompanying glass spoon. But mostly it was the sweet potatoes—never in his life had he had as much of these as he wanted, not with marshmallows on them, not in the place where he came from. And yet, he did strive to eat with politeness, even to wiping off the knife after each use. And did so well, so like an adult . . . Belinda was beaming at him.

"My!" said the mother. "Here Ben, take some of these *persimmons*."

He took one, one only. Never had he cared for these things, stewed or not. That was when he realized that the tiny Thymus was watching him darkly, with detestation in his heart. The mother was watching Thymus.

"Look at you. Been under the house *all day*, playing with them dogs. Makes me mad!"

Again, the biscuits came past, Ben taking two. He liked to scoop out a little "pocket" and then fill it, well-buttered, with further bright green jelly made from quinces.

"He's eating all of 'em!" said Thymus.

"I know it," said the mother. "But it ain't polite to say anything. Hush."

They went out onto the porch, carrying their ice cream with them. Two times, Ben had noticed an old man come halfway down the stairs, and then turn and go back up. Now, with the ice cream having been brought forth, he came down all the way and filled what Ben thought at first might be a chamber pot with a landscape scene painted on it.

It was quiet on the porch, the night still. Here and there Ben could make out the hulking silhouettes of the farm buildings, some of them shifting restlessly, as it seemed to him. He saw an opossum trundling across the yard, until the thing realized that people were watching. Herself, the woman was rocking slowly, her eyes closed. Ben was not sure the father was among them, not until Lucerne said:

"Daddy! Tell about that time."

"He's tired, honey."

"Daddy!"

Moments went by. Ben saw him draw twice at his pipe. Judging by the silence, it was expected that the man would speak very softly, if he agreed to speak at all.

"You don't want to hear about all that again."

It *was* soft, his voice, and seemed to come from far away. Ben too craved to hear the story; he was not, however, inclined to urge the man, nor call him "daddy," nor even to remind them that a stranger from outside the family might be present. Mostly, they were waiting for Thymus to finish with his saucer and spoon. Ben moved nearer. The man's voice put him in mind of dead shucks rattling in the wind.

"Seems like Aunt Lull was sleeping in the *west* room, at that time."

Ben came nearer, Lucerne too; already he could sense the horror of what he was about to hear. Down along the road, a wagon was tacking slowly, its one dull lantern swinging to the ruts.

"Then what happened, Daddy? Daddy?"

"That was Pharis County, not Calauria. You girls don't remember that."

"*I* remember," said Thymus. (His face, Ben saw, was hooded and grim, and in his lap he had the grim head of one of the dogs.)

"Oh you do not. Why, you wern't even born then!"

"*Then* what happened, daddy? Daddy? Daddy!"

"Seems like she just woke up. Sudden-like."

He was telling it correctly; Ben could see the wife and the two daughters, all nodding.

"*Then* what happened? Daddy?"

"This was *Pharis* County, you understand. I doubt it would of happened in Calauria."

"Pharis County," said Belinda, as if in a dream. Suddenly, she bent toward Ben, whispering: "We used to live there."

"*Then* what happened, daddy?"

"Wal! Come to find out, there was a *man* in that room. Just standing there, you understand. Not *doing* nothing."

"He was just standing there, wasn't he daddy?"

"He shore was."

Several moments passed, Ben checking around at each face. "The story's over, I reckon," he said finally.

"Oh Lord no; there's lots more."

"Lots," said Lucerne.

"Yep, seems like she just rolled over, Aunt Lull did. Didn't *say* nothing, you understand. You girls don't remember none of this, of course. Too young."

"*Babies*, is what they were," said Thymus.

"Couldn't *do* nothing."

"Well I reckon not! Not if we was just babies!"

"*Now* we could."

"Oh! *Now* sure. But not *then*."

That was true. Inside, Ben could see the old man climbing slowly up the stairs with his third helping of ice cream. And all this time, it was Belinda wagging one leg happily, her face bright and attentive, her nails chewed to nothing from too much excitement too far prolonged. She loved this time in history—Pharis County; he could read it as much as if she had declared it out loud.

"And *then* what happened, daddy? Hurry! Ben ain't heard it yet."

"Wal!" (He smoked. The voice was softer, and Ben could not be sure it would endure for the remainder of the story.) "Seems like after a while, Lull yelled real loud: 'They's a man in here! They's a man in here!' Didn't do no good, of course."

"It didn't do any good. Did it, daddy?"

"Shore didn't."

"'Cause grandma told her just to roll over, didn't she? Told her just to roll over and go back to sleep. Didn't she, daddy?"

"Shore did. 'Just roll over and go back to sleep.'"

"But she didn't, did she daddy? She didn't just roll over, did she?"

"Not for a long, long time."

"And *then* what happened? Daddy?"

"Wal! Then it was morning."

"Morning!"

"And when they come in . . . Wal! There was branches and leaves and all such, all over the floor!"

"Nigger," said Thymus. "I know it was."

"Leaves, trash. You understand, Ben? It weren't no dream, Aunt Lull was right all the time—there *was* somebody in that west room."

"Whew!" said Ben.

"Nigger. Bound to of been."

"Oh hush up. You weren't even born then!"

"Wal! Anyway, it was all a long time ago."

"*Pharis* County."

"Yep."

Now the story was over, Ben was certain of it. And certain too that it was late and soon he must be on his way, and certain further that he would never have such another day as this one, not if he waited for the world to turn back into a mere nine acres once again. Finally, he stood, and then turned to face them.

"Well, I reckon I'd better get on home now."

"Yep, it's time."

"And I want to thank you for . . ."

"Yes, you've had a big day, for someone like you. Everybody get's *one* like that. But don't you start thinking that . . . !"

"No, ma'am."

"'Cause you only get one. Or maybe two."

"Yes, ma'am." (Belinda had come forward somewhat, but remained behind her mother. He dared to look at her once only, finding that at this late moment she had turned serious, and even sad.)

"Now run on back home now," said the woman. "And careful in this dark!"

He did run, thinking to get back before night turned into outright morning once again. And if once he stumbled, it meant nothing to him. Or would have been nothing, had not he then found himself gazing up to where his burnt quondam mule of old times was spinning still, spinning well, having turned into a mass of stars.

Three

After a certain time, years went by. The county now was so much larger, he thought it might go on forever, reaching past the sun. Fog covered the East, smoke the West, and meanwhile his own father continued to hold in great ignorance the original nine ancient acres (badly worn), together with the fifty-eight that were new. Of these new acres, however, most were thin and already, three times, the plow had broken through. And as if that were not enough, each day now brought Negroes one by one into the county—he saw them morning and night, testing the thickness of the soil that in law belonged to his father only.

Thus Ben. He might labor all day, (his face uncovered), and in the evening run down to the boundary where, clutching at the bars, he might stare over toward that windmill where Belinda used to live. Years passed. Once only, his brother caught him at it, his arm reaching across the boundary. The brother, however, said nothing. For *his* face was largely covered, and his mouth sewed tight.

Other times, he might be plowing in his workmanlike way when, suddenly, he would be struck full in the face with the whiff of honeysuckle. Then it was not unlike him to get down and *roll* in that exultation of May and June to be described in more detail hereinafter. Said to have fed on blooms. In truth, it was plowing that had put him in the way of thinking, and it was thinking that had led on to an excess interest in the sun.

Or, (he was now sixteen), he might come awake at untoward hours and then go crawling among the brothers that still remained, some of whom he recognized and some not, and all suffering from profoundest ignorance. Moaning in the cabin. As to the man his father . . . In this one respect only they both resembled each other very well, namely that neither was any good at sleeping. Ben saw him rise and scowl and draw on both shoes, and then head off to his "altar," there to wait in trembling expectation till sun and thunder drove him back again.

Four

He did give thanks to his good fortune for having come forth in *that* day, and not this one. Cities, (if any then existed), the cities were so small and so far apart, he had perhaps been passing through them all unknowingly while on his way to school. The world was old and he knew it; he could see the evidences of it in every place where the coins and broken pottery peeped out of the ground. But most of all he knew it when after heavy rains a human rib cage might stand revealed with shreds of the original grey uniform adhering to it still.

He gave thanks for not having come forth at a late stage in the on-going development of the county. And yet, unadvanced as he was, he was nobler by far than any other species in the meadow where he spent his days. Loved by the world, loving in return—light, heat, beauty, earth, strangeness, the Alabama sun. And now, here, in morning, the field was long, dark, unsteady, and ringed around with bad-intentioned crickets.

Education, he knew, was hard; moreover, as if it were not awful enough to be as old as he was on this his first day of school, he had also come an hour too early. Three times he circled about the building, twice drawing up quite near to it before, finally, drawing back. In this way he found himself at the bottom of the field, there where the darkness was wont to hang on for as long as possible.

When the sun did come, (dawning with the most amazing suddenness), he lurched forward, pushing between two girls and then entering the room with his face partly covered with one hand. At first, all seemed well, until he saw that one of the students was already so advanced that she had known to bring her own ink. Ben rose to leave; the professor, however, stopped him.

"Ah, Lord. *Benjamin*, is it?"

"Yes, sir."

"Well just set right back down—you ain't going nowhere."

"Yes, sir."

"And just how do you figure on *paying* me, um? I know your daddy hadn't got any money."

"Turnips."

"Lord!"

Ben now gave over the turnips, a full twenty pounds of them in a burlap bag. Already he had locked eyes with a hard-looking boy who, Ben assumed, must derive from the next county. The boy was scuffed, with dust on him, and had one missing finger. Himself, Ben had rather perish than be the first to look away. Could he, or could he not, thrash the whole bunch of them together? That was when he saw that the girl had opened her pot of ink, and that the fluid within it was of the same color as her own gingham dress. The world had *three* dimensions to it—not just night and not just farm; it had also this house of intellect. (Not that the greater part of him wasn't still to be hieing to field or hawing to mule or, on one occasion, ecstasizing face-down in a newly-opened furrow, something he was never to mention to anyone.)

These were his thoughts. He had gnawed down the corner of his book to such an extent, and made drawings in it to such a degree that the girl with the ink was laughing at him. Ben glared. That he could thrash *her*, and very, very easily too . . . She ought to realize it. Suddenly, seeing that the boy from the next county was also staring back, Ben jumped up and took two steps forward, until the teacher came and interposed himself between them.

Education was hard. At times it seemed to Ben that his brain, loaded down now with words, their spelling and their meanings, that his brain might actually crash out through the encompassing bone, killing him. He broke two pencils, so brittle was the graphite, nor did it do him any good to dip them in the ink. His one eye was upon the color of the girl's dress, the other meanwhile looking in increasing despair for that innocent spot that ought to sit behind her ear.

"My father's got sixty acres," he said to her. "Shoot, more than that!"

"Ssssh."

His future wife, she was only nine; Ben looked at her in disappointment. All his life he had wanted to go down to the Edge of the world and sit there with Belinda, and now he knew it would never happen. Suddenly, glancing up, (the boy was grinning in the contemptuous way that Ben could not let pass), he lunged, striking him in the side of the head with his book, and striking so hard that it might have broken the thumb that was still lodged in the pages of that same book. The boy was hard, education too; they rolled, etc., etc.

The day came to an end when afternoon was over. He stepped from the building, his head suffering from education and words, and from a bruise on his upper temple. As to his future wife, he watched her fading off across the field toward the dark tumble-down house where she was known to live with her grandfather, her bell-shaped head just visible above the fennel. Ben had time; he was only sixteen. His wife was only nine. He could wait until the fennel came no higher than her waist, or but little. Now, in one hand he held a book, a gift from the county, and in the other an empty bag previously holding turnips. Time was his, education too. And yet, it still did worry him that he knew no more than he did—he never would—and that never would he be any better than what he would be when he came to be at his best—it worried him.

Five

And then one day he came to town and walked about in it. Never had he viewed so many people, so many exposed faces, so many women, so many girls; quickly, he fell into line and, leading his goat by a string, joined in the promenade that went circulating forever around the courthouse square. It was dignified, it dazzled him; twice he lifted his hat for a woman, both times getting a courteous nod in return. All this he attributed to the extreme youthfulness of the world, and that people were simply not accustomed to seeing such numbers of their own kind. It was on his fifth tour that he passed a white man and two Negroes putting up a building in green lumber and with many a nail being driven wrongly—such was their haste. Ben said nothing. He was of two minds about haste, about Negroes, about life in the city. On the one hand, there was the dignity of it, but on the other, he was ever coming up against boys of his own age and general size who seemed always to be grinning, grinning at *him*, grinning at the string and grinning at the goat.

By afternoon, he knew by rote every tool and object in

every shop window on this side of the courthouse square. And, although it was not always the same on *every* pass, still he had pretty much come to know each face, all the waiters, and the contents of nearly every dish set out on each several table of the enormous hotel restaurant that fronted on the street. He pressed at the glass, striving to get a view into that area where persistent shadows made it difficult to see what was being eaten. There in the extreme rear, he did finally make out a bad man in a hat who had chosen the shadows on purpose and was eating darkly out of a platter of catfish whose tails hung out over the rim. Ben came closer. He knew so little about panes of glass, or that the human vision could cut through it *in both directions*, and that everything his goat did, it was done in full view. Finally a man stepped out onto the walk and coughed twice.

"Ahh . . ."

Ben tried to shake hands with him.

"Your goat there . . ."

"Three dollars," said Ben. "Or, trade him for a shoat."

"'Shoat.'"

"Yes, sir."

"Tell you what, I recommend you try Harvey Gland— that's 'H-A-R-V-E-Y.' That's right. He operates the dry goods store—see it? 'D-R-Y.'" (He pointed. There *was* a dry goods store; moreover, it was on the square.) "Try him! He *likes* goats."

"Think I will."

Now they shook. Inside, at the tables, the men and women seemed to be laughing, wherefore Ben turned, grinned, nodded, waved, and took off his hat. The man with the platter did *not* wave, causing Ben to cast a hard look in his general direction.

The dry goods store, when he came to it, had two Negroes sitting out front on benches. Ben cast a severe look at them, until he came finally to understand that these were *old* men, for the most part, and instead of grinning at the goat, were looking at it sadly.

"Looking for Harvey," said Ben, putting on an authoritative voice. "That's 'H-A-R . . .' He in there?"

"Yasir, 'spec so."

He proceeded inside, but then had to stop for his eyes to adjust. What he saw in front of him was a long narrow corridor with merchandise piled on both sides, and in the rear, several bales of cotton that had been brought in out of the weather and bound in jute. To him, it was much like being in church, owing to the extreme silence, the dust that hung in the air, and the reverential aspect of glass counters holding things of rarity, carefully arranged. And yet, the man himself was small and insignificant, also bald, and had a nasal voice.

"Good God A'mighty, boy; you bring that thing in *here?*"

"Three dollars," said Ben, "and worth it too."

"Pissing on the cotton—I knew he was going to do that. I can always tell."

"Or, trade him for a shoat."

"'Shoat.'"

"Yes, sir."

"You see any shoats in here?"

"No, sir."

"Me neither, I don't see a one. What, did Mobrey send you over here? That's M-O-B . . ."

But already Ben had spotted the bolt of paisley cloth, a dark purple and gold business of such extraordinary complexity that he could read none of it. Hurriedly he unscrolled another two or three yards off the bolt.

"Trade you for this here . . . cloth," said Ben.

"Jesus. Guess I'm going to have to have a talk with that Mobrey. No, no, it hain't got no *smell* to it, for Christ's sakes, it's just *cloth*." He came out now from behind the counter, a small man, and began to look Ben up and down. Dark as it was, he could make out only that the boy was twice his own size, wore rough clothes, and had gone for a very long period without having his hair shorn.

"My stars. You aren't from around *here*, are you?"

"I am too."

"Not one of Vernon's boys?"

Ben admitted that he was.

"Oh! So you been down to the Edge all these years— *now* I understand." He came closer, looking up under the ridges that protected Ben's eyes and kept his hat afloat. "I heard about your brother."

"Dead," said Ben. "Frank's dead too."

"Yes! But you still got lots left, lots. And Vern, is he still working on that . . ."

"Altar, yes sir."

"Hee! One of these days he's going to go so high, he'll . . ."

"Sun, yes sir. How much you asking for that . . . 'terial?"

"'Terial! Well what will you give me for it, hun? Would you give ten acres for it?" (The man came closer, fascinated by what he took to be pure ignorance beneath the rim of the boy's hat.) "Would you give . . . *fifty* acres?"

"I'll give you fifty acres of *land* . . ."

"Yes, yes?""

"For fifty acres of *that*."

The man jumped back. "Been to school, you didn't tell me that. Can you read?"

"I can read writing. Sometimes."

"Is that right? Is that right? What else?"

"Ciphering."

"Is that right?"

"Surveying."

"*That* won't do you no good, not in dry goods. It's the

books you got to be careful with. And I don't care if it's just a penny, you got to mark it down, subtract, add—you understand me, boy? And use ink too—the auditor's real fussy about that."

Ben followed him back between two bales into an especially dark area that held a huge iron safe with a dial on it and, on top, three noble volumes bound in red skin. Ben watched with rapt interest as the man lifted the tallest of them and went splashing through the pages. His glasses had a glint, and Ben was able to see in them the reflection of row upon row of tiny numbers all very neatly inscribed, the ink changing from blue to purple as they came into modern times.

"That's where I stopped," the man said, pointing to the last number of all. "Now! let's see your penmanship."

In fact, the pen itself was large, weighty, and might contain as much as a full quart of ink, judging from it. Ben hoisted it with circumspect and then, looking to the ceiling, thought deeply. He had decided to write down the whole series of numbers from "one" to "nine," and did so, delaying at some length over the "six" and the "seven" especially. The man seemed pleased.

"That's it! There ain't no more! You know about 'zero,' of course."

"Yes, sir."

"Well then! You can help me pack."

Ben followed upstairs. It was a considerable room the man had, equipped both with a bed, a bureau, and a wash stand to boot. At once Ben went to the window, which gave a breathtaking view of the promenade wending its way with tremendous dignity all around the four sides of the courthouse square.

"Yes," said the man, (he was packing feverishly, throwing his things into a tiny valise with a leather strap and buckle to it), "yes, I've spent a lot of time at that window. You will too. And on clear days you can see old man Vernon's tower. Pass me them towels, if you would please. No, keep one for yourself."

Ben followed him down. The goat had gotten into the saddle polish, was eating of it, and by the time Ben managed to tether the creature, the man had gone outside with his suitcase and had moved off some distance before stopping and coming back and squinting in through the screen.

"What church you go to, boy?"

"Sir?"

"Bad, that's bad. They won't buy nothing if you don't show up in church."

"But. . ."

"That don't matter!"

"I knew about 'zeros' even before I learnt about them other ones."

They looked at each other through the screen. It was a bright day, warm, and the promenade now had any number of women in it, some wearing amazing hats. It was the wealth, the women, the plenty, the dignity of it and the number of mules that were so well-behaved that Ben wanted to go and praise them to their faces, one by one. And then too, it was the courthouse which covered acres and ran up and up, carrying a clock so far into the sky that it made him feel doubly strange, strange about time, and strange about the sky.

Six

He went back right away and began to arrange the merchandise. All his life he had had a vocation for systems, for arrangements, for carrying things out to perfection. Here, perfection was far easier in town, far more so than in hieing to field or hawing to mule. Easiness, however, was a sin.

He gave two days to working among the thread, until

he had established a regime in which the more beautiful colors (some never seen before) were well out of reach of anyone who might wish to purchase any of them. He enjoyed standing behind the counter in darkness, watching as the blue-green flies went tumbling head over heels, playing exuberantly in the shafts of light. Or, he might spread out one or another of the paisley rolls and then, locking the door and pulling the blinds, get down on all fours and try to decipher the future in it. No one had to know that he also used paisley in lieu of sheets.

Or, sometimes, he might fling open the back door and look down the long, narrow, fenced strip that ran all the way to the river and beyond, where already a few shacks were going up on the opposite coast. It was here, here in the free time between customers that he installed his garden, itself also long and narrow and arranged alphabetically by the name of the crop. And if now the town had a full thousand souls in it, yet was he nevertheless able to tend a goat and possess a hive of bees. Weeks passed, the number of customers growing fewer and fewer even as the dry goods themselves became better and better organized and stored higher and higher out of reach. And during all this time he received but one letter only, a brief message in a trembling hand that described how the lizard, devastated by Ben's departure, was losing its scales.

In the second year, he began to go out on promenades of his own. To be sure, it still did give him an odd feeling, life in the city, and to be forever meeting up with yet another unfamiliar face that gave no real inkling about what the underlying person might be thinking—the town was full of these. Then he would fly back to the store and close and lock the doors. Rainy days especially, that was when he retreated all the way to his attic and, for as long as the weather endured, would sit looking across into other windows on the three sides of the square. He saw, first, a group of men whispering together in the hotel lobby. He saw, secondly, the confederate statue, the face contorted in the agony of battle and of rust. He saw into the courthouse fountain, where the several dozen giant goldfish had come together as if for warmth. He saw into the barber's shop, the barber himself asleep upon his throne. Mules he saw, mules winking to one another around the square, all of them soon to enjoy a rendezvous in paradise. He saw where that girl who lived on the fourth floor of the hotel, how she came running out to bring in the washing, the same washing that just an hour ago she had hung out to dry. But most of all he could see a windmill, ten miles off, and a hundred yards beyond that, a bending tower made of shells and mica, each day a little taller.

He made coffee and paced about the room. From his other window, he could keep a steady surveillance upon the river, now boiling in fog. It could go on raining for days. Or, this precipitation might lift within the hour, giving way to evening heat. (There still was a very great perturbation in the upper atmosphere, and no likelihood that it would settle during *his* lifetime, not in *this* particular county.) He saw the goldfish, saw their little faces smiling with terror. It could not be moisture they dreaded. It must therefore be lightning.

He smoked, a transgression that he allowed himself now and again, when the weather was like this. He worried for his garden, his bees, for his father lying unsleepingly beneath a punctured roof. And if now the county had far more acreage to it, and the square had four sides, and each side had five, sometimes six buildings to it, and each building sometimes three stories or more, yet was he nevertheless confident that in time such rains would come to wear it all away again and render things back unto what they used to be, and should be, which is to say nine acres only, a few brothers, and the Edge of the world.

Twice he went down to check on the merchandise. In the garden, his squashes were threatening to float away. His bee skep, on the other hand, was water-tight, and inside it—and he could hear this quite plainly—the hundreds of laborers had come together in a vast crowd to sing praises to the King. He *tried* to get a look at it, but the entrance was tight, and well-guarded indeed.

It was toward three in the afternoon that his aunt came in and began dancing about the floor, fighting with her hat, her galoshes, and a parasol designed to hold off, not rain, but sun and light only. He had seen this before, having seen her in the country and seen her in church. He had *never* seen her wet.

"So! Smoking again—I can tell. Well? Are you going to fetch me a towel, or not? No, I need to know."

Ben fetched. He was pleased to see her of course, but not today, not in weather that he preferred to use for his thinking.

"Whew!" he said. "Howdy."

"Yes, you sound like your father. Oh, he's a great one, when it comes to not saying anything. And I suppose he's lying out there right now, rain splashing in his face."

"Yes, ma'am."

"And Lloyd?"

"Yes, ma'am. He left."

"Well! That's *one* good thing. And you, you got yourself a real *position* here—is that what you think?"

"Yes, ma'am."

She laughed, Ben joining in. This was an educated woman, one could see it in her scarf and flowers, her parasol, and her rueful hesitation when he brought up the split-bottom chair and offered it to her. Two minutes went past while she adjusted herself. Ben preferred to sit, thirty feet away, in the footwear department, in the good leathern smell that invested that area. (The woman had chosen to stay where the more subtle odor of mere linseed oil prevailed.) It was dark in the store. Now came the cat, fat and yellow; time and again it continued to jump up into her lap, until finally she permitted it to stay. Very soon now Ben would hear the old stories—it was for this and nothing else that she had ventured out in such weather in the first place. He waited for them. Should he, or should he not, ignite the lantern? No, not unless he wished to draw customers during the stories.

"You've heard all that old business about your grandfather Frixtus and that pig."

"Yes, ma'am."

"Today then we'll talk about other things."

"Yes, ma'am. Tell about . . ."

"No, no, no, no. No! You've heard enough about that, no. Today we'll talk about the trouble between Enterprise and Opp."

He waited for it. He knew so little about those days, a few weird remarks his father had let slip, before his father had given up on talk. And then too, he questioned why only the past had yielded such peculiar stories, and in his own day, nothing worth telling about. She said:

"You should know that your great, great grandfather—and I do hope you will guard yourself against this, Ben, should you find the same tendency in yourself—was a wrathful man. No patience, none, no forbearance, nothing like that, oh no. I expect that's why he left Maryland in the first place—some old feud belike. Why, you have only to look at a map to see how it was in those days—I mean!—what with all those blank spaces. They had no way of knowing even where the counties stopped and where they started. How would *you* like it? Well, you can't blame 'em, the instruments they had." (Here she paused, the cat having stood up tall in her lap in order to search her in the face.) "But Ben! you should know too that he didn't come straightway *here*, no. Oh no, first he had to try it out in *Connecuh* County, and nothing in the world down there but thistles and sand niggers and the like. Well! Impossible to *grow* anything, in dirt like that."

Ben nodded. He could visualize that soil, the great heat, and the exasperation of trying to plow in mere sand. He was glad for it when his ancestor decided to leave. "Tell about . . ."

"I'm coming to that. I declare, you're as bad as him! So all-fired impatient. Alright: His first wife, she . . ."

"Scalped," said Ben.

"Yes."

"Scalped by the Greeks."

"*Creeks*, Ben."

He knew the story well, how that the woman who might almost have been his own great, great grandmother, how she had been dealt with by Indians while on her journey to Calauria. Everything that he had, he had given it all and gladly to have been there, the chance to safeguard this woman, reported to have been so small.

"They did it."

"Yes they did. But we can't worry about that *now*, Ben. You hear me?"

Ben sat. The day was darker, the rain fierce. Outside, he saw a bird that had been killed by it, drowned among his squashes.

"Tell about . . ."

"I'm coming to that. Alright, here it is: After all those troubles and so forth, one thing and another . . ."

"He came here!"

"Yes. You like that part, don't you Ben?"

"Yes, ma'am."

"You're thinking it right now. Aren't you?"

"Yes, ma'am. Was it raining?"

"Like today? Well, lands! *I* don't know. It *might* have been raining."

"They couldn't see where they were, raining like that. No courthouse *then*, I don't reckon. Was there?"

"I wouldn't think so, no."

"No courthouse, no bridges. Whew! And when it quit raining . . ."

"Yes?"

"Well then they could see where they were. They saw it was *here*. I reckon it was a big shock alright, after traveling all that way."

"Now *you're* telling about it, and *I'm* just listening."

"How many was there? There was Newton, there was Lewis. There was Mary too."

"Yes."

"There was Matthew."

"That's correct. And you, were you there too, Ben?"

"And Victoria, she was only two years old. Now first, they had to clear away the scorpions and so forth. Vipers."

"No, no, no; that's the *Bible*, Ben. You just let your imagination run all away with you. Why, Ben? Because your father's crazy too? No, no, that was *good* soil. And then, they had 410 acres in those days."

"Before grandaddy 'drank it all away'?"

"That is correct."

They looked at each other. In his thoughts, he had a picture of those earlier times and of his great grandfather's cabin full of his grandfather and grandfather's brothers, all of them drinking in great darkness with faces covered. It had been a time of widespread ignorance, and yet he regretted the passing of it, and the long, long wait before he would be enabled to gaze upon the face of Mary and Newton, and the two-year-old who had died too soon.

"Aunt Xenia?"

"Yes?"
"Nothing."

In the late afternoon, he had but two customers only, neither of them tarrying for very long. Finally, toward six, the rain yet heavier and greyer and threatening to settle in permanently, he made coffee. Across the square, he could make out two feeble lights, one of them sputtering badly and the other, apparently, a mere candle. His aunt had scarcely moved, save to take off her hat and shake it out, and then put it back on again. He knew so little about her true character, and why she might wish to visit *him*, the offspring of a father whom she so despised. Finally, toward seven, with thunder moving over, he asked the question that had been pestering at him for several days.

"Aunt Xenia?"
"Yes? I can't see you."
"I shore do wish you would consider it—picnic on Sunday. Would you? Me and that gal over to the rooming house?"
She almost spilled her coffee. "That skinny girl?"
"Yes, ma'am."
"Why, Benjamin Reuben! But she's very skinny, Ben."
"I don't care."
"And her *mother* . . ."
"Her mother is just as good as my daddy."
That was true.
"That's true. Better! But then everybody's better than that."
"Would you?"
"Chaperone?"
"Yes, ma'am."
"At the hanging?"
"No, ma'am; that's going to be *Saturday*. I'm talking Sunday."

"But Benjamin! You know we don't go to that church."

"That don't matter! We can go *once*, I reckon."

"But Ben! She isn't even from this part of the county."

"That don't matter!" Then: "Well what part *is* she from?"

"You're a study, boy. When did you ask her?"

"*You* could ask her."

That night, it rained again. In his upstairs room he had, (among many other things), a number of books, of which far the most important was the *Report of the Commissioner of Agriculture for the year 1865*. Ben now lifted it gingerly in both hands and spread it on the table. As to the actual commissioner himself, he who once had known so much . . . Ben's thoughts flew back to that bright day in early '66 when the man must have posed in great pride beside his pile of freshly-printed books. Where now was that man? So much knowledge, so much, such wisdom, so many illustrations, such tiny, tiny print; looking into it more closely, Ben informed himself of the quantity in 1860 of the Vermont cheese production. And yet all this was as nothing however, when set down beside the *Observations on Atmospheric Humidity* submitted by J. S. Lippincott of Haddenfield, New Jersey—Ben need only to glance through the essay, addressed to a "large and intelligent class of readers," to confirm that in the preceding generation the intelligent class of readers had been large. And yet, he would never visit Haddenfield himself, never, no, nor shake the hand of Lippincott, that large and intelligent man. In any case—and he based this judgement upon the yellow and brittle quality of the pages themselves—the man was probably dead by now.

One full hour, he lay in darkness, hoping that the rain *would* come back, this time to stay. He had never been

any sort for sleeping, his father neither nor, (Ben liked to
believe), not Mary nor Newton nor any of those others
currently beneath ground in a far distant part of the
county where they lay, each of them looking up unblink-
ingly at a very low lid that nearly touched the nose.

It was all too much, too low; Ben jumped out of bed
and, lifting the lamp, went down to check on the merchandise. Outside, a bee-eating blackbird had come to
roost upon the skep itself, quite prepared to wait five
hours for the day. His squashes had *not*, however, drifted
away; Ben shined the light on them, finding they had actually profited from the rain. Moon too, the thing was
dim in parts, and yet still easily able to lord it over every
other bright star.

Keeping the lantern on lowest flame, he left the shop
and began again, the ten thousandth time he had done
so, to move about the square. Could anything be more
strange than this, how that at certain hours the people of
this town were wont to draw off into specialized chambers, there to lie in amazement for full seven hours till
dawn itself and its manifold roosters bade them rise
again, and again set to labors? No! But perhaps he too
should be sleeping—the night was sweet enough. Or
perhaps he was being followed—certain old-world
shades. In any case, this time in history was beginning to
seem to him most peculiar indeed.

It was a time when the town had *two* lawyers in it,
one of them large and the other quite small. This night,
the greater of them was working past hours in his upstairs office where Ben could very clearly see his bird-like
profile pasted to the window shade. He was an astute
man, famous for his cautiousness, and for being cau-
tiously corrupt. Ben, who had no wish whatsoever to
alert the man, tiptoed past, shielding his lantern. As always, the courthouse itself was open, and he was able to

make out two drunks loitering in the corridor. He elected therefore not to cut through the building, not at this time. (For he had never forgotten how on just such a night as this one, a certain locally-famous wild hog had taken up in the office of Clerk of Court, wounding several.)

He went on, smoking, talking to himself, and then crossing finally in front of the four wan Negroes still sitting out on the bench in front of Dagon's place. He knew them well, and knew too how that after thirty years not one of them had ever yet seen, nor heard, nor spoken, nor yet smelt of evil. Tonight it was late, the Negroes tired, and as he drew closer Ben saw how the four were sharing one single pair of eyeglasses, fighting for it among themselves. *He'd* not be the one to deprive them of it, snatching it away like the children of the town. On the contrary, Ben slowed and lifted his hat, but then had to wait a minute for all four to acknowledge what he was doing.

He went around twice more, past the livery and the empty space, past the rooming house and his own dry goods shop, and then again past the lawyer's office in which the man himself, or his profile rather, seemed to be bending ever closer toward the window, as if to inspect a fly.

He went out into the country, three o'clock in the morning. It was not far and yet, when he looked behind, he saw that he had left a trail of unsteady prints in the powder that led all the way back to town. And when he looked away, (glancing toward the woods), it seemed to him that the town itself went out of existence during that short interval—until, of course, he looked again. No doubt about it, God's Hand was much quicker than any eye of *his*. Next, he passed three mules confined to a pen, serene creatures who kept their opinions under strict and courteous control. Ben loved to encroach upon them and to peer deeply into each of their six eyes, each eye reflecting back a slightly variant prospect of the pock-marked moon.

He continued on, passing by a line of abandoned shacks. To south, he saw a listing shape, tenuous and bending and far too tall to be as slender as it was, and every night a little taller. Itself, the moon was great, calm, benign, huger than the world—he would have leapt to it, if he could. He spied a long procession of crows winging homeward toward it in stately order. Next came the river twining back and forth across his route, its contents having altered into a thin red wine full of intoxicated breams and several eels. He saw quantities of frogs all standing shoulder to shoulder, gargling with the stuff. Here too he came into a stand of pines, a dignified species grieving over one of their own number who had recently fallen. And that was when he saw something that made him come to a sudden halt, and even go back for a few paces—a very old couple picking their way hand in hand through the woods. Ben was shocked; never had he seen the likes of this, people so old and at such an hour in the morning. And now they have taken off their very old clothes, and now they kiss, and now were bathing in the wine!

Seven

Sunday did come, bringing brightness; twice, (dressed in his suit), he went outside to check on it. In the eyes of the bees, sunlight turned everything to rapture. Their little doorway, however, was too small for the traffic, such was their enthusiasm for carrying out the behests of their King. And then Ben noticed how a passion flower had gotten mixed up in the squashes and was letting off its own peculiar scent.

He had expected to see the girl being led on toward him across the square by Aunt Xenia; he had *never* thought to see her being brought on by the little Negro boy called sometimes "Grady," and sometimes "Memnon," and sometimes, (by his own family), called "John." Ben came out, gaping as they drew on. He felt so absolutely foolish. His suit, a black garment that barked out loud with each step, it was foolish too, as was indeed his hair, so full of dressing and of oils. Now, moving with elaboration, he held out the passion flower to the girl, but then quickly pulled it back in again when he realized that she was still some distance off.

"Xenia can't come!" said Memnon.

Ben nodded. He knew enough to know that it was better to go on talking for a great while, and not to try and *hold* her all at once. He did recognize that she was dressed in yellow and, with the adroitness of her kind, had on a yellow bonnet as well.

"Howdy!" he yelled. "I figured we'd go to the *picnic,* if that's what you really want."

They were moving quickly, straight back across the square. She wouldn't allow him to see very much of her face. He did observe that her hands were very nearly as big as his own, and that she took long strides, as if she were going across a field with furrows; he and Grady both were having trouble staying up with her.

"How come you picked *me?*"

Ben shrugged. He would have described the voice as slightly deeper than to be expected, and slightly hoarse. He liked it however.

"I seen you hanging out wash."

"Oh."

"But don't worry; I ain't going to *do* nothing."

"No, ma'am; he ain't going to do *nothing.*"

"Nothing," said Ben. "Talk, maybe. But that's all."

The girl blushed. That was when he caught sight of her nearer eye, a blue flash, hardly half a second's worth, the first blue flashing eye Ben had ever observed. This eye, with its speed, it had given itself very little time to see all that it needed to know of *him*. How he loathed his suit, the jelly in his hair, the red clay ignorance that shone in his uncovered face!

Quickly they passed by Dagon's place where the four faded Negroes watched with an intense interest that turned to outright wheezing and laughter and a contest for their one set of eyeglasses when John came racing past. Ben could see the girl's hand, could see it swinging in and out of view, though he durst not himself grab for it as yet. He also caught the smell of her perfume, a queer, strange, faint, and very far away scent that puzzled and worried him, and inspired him to walk faster.

The cows had all been moved away to other fields, making room for the singing. It was not his church, the girl's neither; it *was*, however, the finest singing choir in the county. Among them, Ben saw a tall woman, taller than the men, whose voice was the best of all. And yet, just next to her was one who had forgotten the words and now was merely humming. They moved closer, Ben, Memnon, and the girl.

"I reckon you do lots of singing," said Ben loudly. "At church. *Your* church, I mean. Do you?"

She blushed, looked down, squinted, and then stared off into the far-away mountains. Again, he felt a keen desire to *hold* her just now, and would have done so, could he have brought it off without her knowing about it. Her dress was yellow indeed, and crisp, and had the sort of extreme cleanliness that he expected of someone so good at washing and hanging out clothes. Suddenly, she shot another look at him with that lightning quickness, the second such time she had done it. Fifty feet away, Memnon was watching darkly.

"Pshaw," said Ben, "I can sing a *hundred* hymns, near about. And not even looking at the words!" But then it occurred to him that she might be tired. He knew so little about women and girls.

"You want to go set for a while? Shoot, just tell me if you do!"

She didn't. Now, taking her by the hand, an action that alarmed Grady but that also seemed to happen of itself, he led her off, the two of them stepping delicately between the families sprawled here and there on their blankets. Very few Negroes; Ben had to assume they were staying in their cabins, still meditating on yesterday's hanging. Ahead, at the top of the knoll, he spotted the photographer's tent, and out front the man himself with his tripod, his enormous camera, and his painted scenes. They stayed to watch one of the corn farmers have his portrait taken in front of a canvas that pictured the interior of an office with a massive desk and shelves laden down with books.

They went on, passing by a booth in which three women were giving a demonstration on improved methods for canning fruits and vegetables. Ben saw the dentist, a portly man who had brought his gear with him; here too half a dozen farmers had formed up in line, some to be treated and some, the larger number of them, simply to watch.

"Shoot," said Ben, "you want to go over yonder? Watch that there *dentist*?"

"I reckon not."

(It was the third time he had heard her voice. It confirmed what he remembered of it from the first time.)

"You sound just like . . . Say it again: 'Reckon not.'"

"No!" (She pulled back.) "What in the world's the matter with you?" (But she was grinning.)

"'Reckon not, reckon not, reckon not.'" That was when

he made his grab for her. People were smiling, and meanwhile she was trying to hit him on the arm. He would not have thought it possible, that she who only five minutes ago had been unwilling to look him in the face, that now she was trying to hit him on the arm. He had a tremendous wish to tickle her about the ribs, which were lean, and which put him in mind of his lizard's—he could see them sheathed beneath the dress.

"No, Mr. Ben!" (Grady speaking.)

"I'm going to fetch you up there, so that there 'dentist' . . ."

"You are not."

"You don't need all them teeth anyway."

He had to chase her, she was fast. John too was fast, and better able than either of them to leap over the people on their blankets. The singing had meanwhile started up again, this time accompanied by an accordion and harp.

Ben did catch her finally, but as to whether she was angry, embarrassed, afraid, delighted . . . He never could be sure when it came to girls.

"Want your picture taken?"

"No!"

"Shoot, it won't hurt! Me, I've had *my* picture taken hundreds of times. Hey! You want to win some money?"

She looked at him curiously at first, but then gave one of her quick glances to the man in the booth, a lofty-looking person in full suit and a tie decorated with emblems of dollar bills. Thus far, no one had dared to deal with this person, not so far as Ben had seen. Moreover, the man appeared to be gazing straight ahead, peering dreamily into the furtherest future, and liking what he saw. At once Ben went up to the counter, took out a dime, and slapped it down under his nose.

"Don't do it, Mr. Ben!"

Farmers gathered around, all of them grinning.

"Ah!" said the man. (His voice was clear, educated too.) "So it's a wager you're offering me?"

"I do. I am, I mean." On the counter, not ten inches away, Ben saw three walnut shells of the ordinary kind. *These* shells, however, had little human faces painted on them, of which two were smiling gladly, but the other was all in tears. Slowly, very slowly, the man now lifted the middle-most shell, raising it just high enough, (but no higher), to show the pea.

"Is there, or is there not—I put it to you—a tiny green pea beneath the face that is smiling?"

Ben nodded. But then, seeing that nodding was not enough, he said: "Yes, sir; I seen it. I seen the pea."

"Don't do it, Mr. Ben!"

"Very well! I too, I have seen the pea. And now I must ask you to keep your eye on it—that's my advice. Oh, I'll go slowly."

And did go slowly. Ben was wise enough to watch, not the man, but the smiling shell that bore the pea. Six moves and no more, all of them deliberate and slow.

"Good enough! And now, my friend, I can see by looking at you that you're not so easily fooled. Are you?"

Ben grinned. "No, sir."

"You know, don't you? You know where the pea is."

"I do; yes, sir."

The man groaned, sighed deeply, and then took out a dime of his own and set it next to Ben's. "Very well, take it, take it, take it, it's yours. You earned it."

"Hey! Ain't you . . . ?"

"Mr. Ben!"

"Ain't you going to *test* me?"

"Why should I do that? I believe you." They looked at each other for a long time, until finally, reluctantly, the man weakened and gave in to him at last: "Oh very well then, if you wish, if you wish."

"Mr. Ben!"

Ben leapt to it, springing upon the happy shell that
was somewhat to the right of the man, but yet somewhat
to the left of Ben. Gleefully, he . . . But the pea was not
there! His hand trembled; laughter came from the six
farmers; the girl was tugging at him to come away. Instead, Ben drew nearer, watching as the man employed
two of his larger fingers, which he moistened, and which
he used to take up the two dimes.

"I'm embarrassed," he said. "Embarrassed for *me*.
Clearly, what we've just seen here today is a disconjunc-
tion of some kind. Most unusual. I can't believe it would
happen again."

"Me neither, I can't believe it neither."

"So."

"Let's go over yonder," said the girl. "They've got ice
tea."

"Now just hold on," said Ben. "I'm not afraid of any
'junction anyway, and anyway I've got *lots* of dimes." (He
took one now and slapped it down.)

"Mr. Ben!"

The tea, when they came to it . . . In fact, the ice had
mostly melted by now and the fluid had a small brown
toad in it with its head sticking out. Ben drank off two
cups at once, allowing the girl to pay for it. He was in a
dark frame of mind, a frame that darkened even further
when he was approached by a gawky-looking farm boy
with jutting teeth who was vending hot mince pies from
a cupboard suspended around his neck. Hot were the
pies, and had each little fork holes from which the steam
was leaking out.

"Not me," said Ben. "I ain't got any money—
somebody else got it all—and so you might just as well
go pester somebody else."

"I got a nickel, Mr. Ben."

The girl tugged at him. "We could set for a while."

Ben followed, musing on his lost coins. Always there was some little something to keep any given day from being perfect. And then too, he had had his perfect day, long ago, and knew not to ask for more. Suddenly, he dashed forward, hoping to put himself between the girl and a roped-off area where the farmers were fighting a trained hog against two dogs.

They came to the creek and settled there among some half-dozen other couples who had thought to bring quilts with them. Here, he saw an example of a man who seemed to be sleeping, his head resting peacefully in a woman's lap. As to what sort of experience this might be, to have one's head in the very lap of a woman, Ben could not well imagine. Nor, with Memnon squeezed in between them, nor could he and the girl be said to form a "couple." Instead, Ben smoked, doing it brazenly. On the platform, the men's chorus was singing noisily, some of them having gone red in the face; they lacked, however, the extreme spiritual conviction of their wives in such matters. And if some of the families were already loading their wagons and making ready to depart, yet still others were only just now coming in. A boy strolled by, (leading a cow by a string), followed by a mental defective with no funds who stood gaping at the booths. Here, close by the creek, Ben felt a sudden wish to sleep, and to do it with his head in the lap of the girl. Again, he saw her glance at him, and again look away.

"Hell, I ain't going to hurt you."

"He ain't going to hurt you."

"*Hold* you, is all, and I ain't even going to do that."

She looked off into the mountains, there where the horizon was flickering between blue and grey and the trees were like a furze of corduroy. Ben grinned at her. He was on the verge of saying something to her, until distracted by a dragonfly that came to a stance at just that moment on his knee. To his thinking, these were the oddest of all creatures on earth, the cruelest too, to judge by their looks. Using his empty tea jar, he trapped the thing under glass.

"Oh!"

"Shoot, that's nothing. Why, I've caught hundreds of these things. See that neck?"

She bent closer, looking at the neck. The head itself was gorgeous, variegated, and huge in proportion, all of it attached by a mere thin "wire," as opposed to any normal sort of neck at all. Himself, Ben was gazing at the neck of the girl.

"How can they *swallow*?"

"They do. Hell, I don't know."

"And look at all them colors! How come they're so fancy?"

"They just like it that way, I reckon."

"Are you going to let her go?"

"'Her'?"

"So she can go home to her babies?"

"There ain't no babies! Hey, you want me to *eat* her?"

"No!"

"Shoot, all you have to do is . . ."

But in fact the thing flew away. He grabbed for it, missing. It was enough to incite John to leap up and go chasing after it. And now that they were alone at last, and at last a couple in the true sense . . . Ben edged closer, grinning. Her perfume had not yet entirely evaporated; moreover, her neck was thinner, and her dress more brightly yellow, than he had realized. The inspiration came to him to rest his head in her lap.

"If I could just . . ."

"No! Gracious. Oh listen—they're singing again. And here comes Grady back too, see?"

She was humming rapidly now, but also halting every so often to give him an anxious glance. She *was* herself, no doubt about it, a person in her own right, discrete and contained, and quite distinct from *him*self in both space and time. *He,* on the other hand, was a force; this was what worried her. Again he grinned, edging closer. He knew enough about himself to know that, given time enough and good weather, he could wear all such stubbornness down to dust.

He woke; the night was clear and splashed with innumerable white spiny stars that looked like asterisks. (His mind flew back to that great man, the long-defunct Lippincott of Haddenfield, the first in the world to have appreciated the real effects upon the human vision of just such atmospheric disconjunctions as this one.) The farmers meanwhile, most of them, had taken up their horse-blankets, their baskets, and their prizes, and were wending off in their wagons, carrying their reluctant daughters with them. It was mostly the townspeople who remained now, those who could afford to stay out late. For *their* homes were only rods away, instead of miles.

He found the girl—Grady had gone off after the fly and had not come back—found her down by the stream.

"Reckon I went to sleep!" he said, snorting at himself. "And now it's all dark everywhere, with them big white stars." (He pointed.) "Where's the people?"

There *were* people. He saw Seth, Seth the banker, a fifty-year-old man, saw him rise and stretch and then go trudging off into the woods, carrying a little satchel with him. Gone now was the photographer's booth, gone the dentist, and gone all the tents save one. Gone was the scoundrel with his pea and faces. Ben turned to the girl; she had been reading the creek so long, and perhaps the stars as well, that she had lapsed into a "brown study," as Xenia might have said.

"What's the matter!"

"Oh, nothing."

"Shoot, you can tell *me.*"

"Everybody's leaving."

Now he understood. "And because they'll all be dead and gone someday?"

She nodded.

"And nobody will remember that we had a picnic to-day?"

She nodded. He too, for some time now the suspicion had been building in him that the future might not greatly care about this county, and especially not now that there were so many others just like it, all of them lined up shoulder-to-shoulder across the whole state. He edged closer. Perhaps if he should *hold* her just now, perhaps it would be something they could remember in-to those remote times when they both would be old, and the county abandoned, forgotten, and spinning through space. He came closer.

"If I could just . . ."

No, there was a sudden activity on the knoll. It sur-prised him to see some dozen or more of the older peo-ple, the town's most notable, and including both lawyers, to see them disappearing into the edge of the woods, on-ly then to emerge shortly thereafter dressed in their fin-est clothes. The choir was much smaller, only five voic-es—the music was weak.

"We ought to leave," said Ben. "But first, let's wait. Will that be alright?"

She nodded. Seth, he saw, had come forth from the woods in his high hat, wearing a lugubrious look. As to what manner of theological procession was in prepara-tion . . . Ben could not imagine. He saw the surveyor, a man with but seven fingers, saw him, saw the Deacon, saw the jailer, saw them all line up precisely behind Seth.

"We ain't supposed to be here!"

"Hush," said Ben.

It was remarkable: The singing had hardly come down to its end before some dozen figures, all of them dressed up like Death, (flour on their faces), issued suddenly out of the forest and came forward to link hands with Seth and his followers. Ben gasped. Each foremost citizen now had a ghost-like partner at his side, and each ghost his own citizen. Ben saw one wearing a necklace comprised of the vertebrae of cattle, and then two others holding up horses' skulls in front of their faces. It was morose music indeed now being sung, broken once by a shrill trumpet. The girl was stunned, terrified, silent. Himself, Ben believed he knew what it was, and why Memnon had left— how that each man's partner was to emblemize the ghost that the man himself must shortly become. It did not seem so awful; Ben was almost ready to say that it was a fit ending to an amazing day. Or *would* have said it, had they not then started in on their filthy little dance, with rattles and spears.

Eight

Sometimes, sitting by his upstairs window, he liked to reflect back upon his days in education, his six weeks of '84, and the further time of '87. To his great shame, he had packed away the commissioner's *Report* among his own belongings, treating it as if the thing were his own legal possession instead of the store owner's. Or, sometimes, sitting by the window, (thinking and smoking), he might see the girl come out of the rooming house carrying a bundle of laundry. Moments like that, he would press at the glass, striving to cut the distance between them by a few inches, there to await the moment when she would give a quick blue glance, faster than thought, toward the second-story window of the dry goods store.

Or—and he was *never* any good at sleeping—he might rise during the worst part of the night, light the lantern, and then refer back to the European Grape Disease of 1845, a most brilliant essay illustrated by woodcut en-

graving plates of some of the actual spores. True, some of
the conclusions seemed not altogether to apply, not in
Alabama, or anyway not in those Alabama parts of which
he had actual first-hand cognizance, finding no grapes
anywhere. In his own garden, certainly, he allowed no
spores, none, sometimes even rising during those worst
parts of the night in order to go outside and shoo them
away.

It happened one day when he was in his garden that
he came upon a certain growth that was too large, too
soft—it absolutely nauseated him—and too much like an
internal human organ. At once he tossed it away from
himself, where it landed with a grunt. Unfortunately, it
also left a wound in the garden, and at the bottom of it a
little fund of seepage that looked like blood. Ben was
pondering it, even at one moment dipping the corner of
his handkerchief into the stuff when, suddenly, he became aware that a person in shoes was standing just next
to him.

"Howdy," Ben said.

"Yes indeed."

"Turnips!"

"Yes, nauseating. You was still lying in *bed*, B. R., the
first time I came by. Talking to yourself! I don't know
about you, boy—most folks try to get their sleeping done
at *night*."

"I got some coffee on."

They went inside. Benjamin knew this man, a digni-
tary with suits and cattle, and acres in the West.

"Well," said Ben, "if I was talking in my sleep, it might
be because . . ."

"Good, good, yes. Now I'm offering you a job, Ben, if
you want it. Now you're a real good *speller*, isn't that so?
Well I'm offering you a job in spelling."

Ben dropped two turnips. One rolled beneath the bed.

"Job."

"Oh yes indeed."

"But . . ."

"That don't matter! Well? You want it?"

"But . . ."

"They'll pay you! Now if they *don't* pay you, well then I'd quit, if I was you."

"But . . ."

"Shore! We *need* good-spelling people in this county. Now where would I be if *I* couldn't spell real good?"

"I don't know."

"See? Well, you want it?"

Ben looked down. He had never been any sort of speller, even if he did know a number of words.

"I need to . . . lucubrate about this."

"See? See what I mean about you? Oh, you're going to be a *fine* speller!"

"Cogitate."

"See?"

They shook. It needed only a moment to retrieve the turnip from under his bed, but when he came up, the supervisor was gone.

At noon, he closed the store and went over to the fountain where the girl sat waiting for him.

"Well," (he said), "seems like I'm a teacher now."

"Teacher!"

"Oh yes absolutely. You know it as well as I do—we *need* good-spelling people in this county. We can get married now, I reckon."

"Married!"

"Oh, I'm not saying I'll do it for free. Hell, if they don't pay me, shoot I'll just . . ."

"But we're moving away, mamma and me."

"Now what did you just say?"

"So I don't see how we can get married."

Her eye, normally so unable to meet his, now it had a wild look. Ben came closer. She was so thin, so pale, had so little to say, and the state was so large, the counties so numberless—let her get only so far out of town and, he knew it, he'd never be able to find her again.

"You ain't going anywhere. And so there's no need to even talk about it." He stood, stretched, and then sat again. "And what do you mean, 'moving away'?"

"To Hermione. That's where daddy is."

"Daddy."

"He wants us back."

"Well I reckon he does! Too late now."

"We have the letter."

"Why Lord, I don't put any stock in letters! You shouldn't either. And anyway, shoot, I could *walk* to Hermione, if I had to. Shoot, I can walk *hundreds* of miles."

She looked at him in tremendous admiration. "Hundreds! Anyway, it's only thirty miles."

"Thirty!" He snorted, and then suddenly leapt up and walked off a few paces and then came back, to show his hiking style. "Good Lord, thirty miles, shoot, that ain't *nothing*; makes me mad just to talk about it."

"I believe you could walk to the moon, if you had to."

Ben agreed. She was sitting in just such a way that he could almost have held her in his arms, except for the presence of the encompassing town with its noise and curiosity, the Confederate statue with its rotting face, and except for the four weird Negroes who seemed actually to expect something of that sort to happen and were waiting for it, fighting for the glasses.

"I shore would like to . . ."

"No!" Then: "But I'll be fifteen next month."

"That don't matter! Shoot, my grandmother was *seventeen* before they . . . Shoot, I can wait."

She smiled at him gratefully, even as the four Negroes

lapsed back into their mid-day lethargy. For ten minutes Ben sat side by side with her, until a mule came passing by in whose deep brown eye they saw themselves sitting side by side watching a mule passing by.

That night, he strolled again down into the country-side, his face set in the general direction of that same "Troezen County" that made such a disfigurement on Alabama's otherwise rather symmetrical map. He did *not*, however, permit himself to transgress the boundary, nor to set down his foot on such alien lands that, in any case, had lost its population many long years ago, owing to the eruptions. Now all was quiet, nor could he discern even so much as a few lingering sparks among the tangled foliage. And here he stayed, musing until three, whereupon at last he turned and began to dance down the boundary toward a bank of dark blue clouds wearing worried expressions.

He did sometimes wish that it were further along in the history of the world, and that he had come forth into more advanced times, when mere cows and crops and stuff as crude as wooden wagons were to be found in old commissioner *Reports*, and there alone. Suddenly, just then, the moon broke free, showing that he was being followed by a full dozen dogs who stopped when he stopped, and who looked up to him in love and admiration. They knew each other well; he could command them with a gesture. Together they now treaded their way down to the river and stood speculating upon that slowly-grinding pool where lately a certain old couple had come hand-in-hand in order to put an end to themselves.

He saw what he thought to be a monstrous trout slumbering in entire innocence, and doing it much too close to the surface for its own good. Ben came nearer. To hoist the thing from its native milieu and then to

have to wrestle with it on shore . . . No. And then too, it
might be one of those salt sea fish who, sickened by the
ferocity that prevailed in those realms, had simply retreated this far up-river in order to grab off one night of
decent sleep. Now, without bothering to take off his
shoes, Ben waded closer, moving in extreme slowness
and then, suddenly, striking a match and holding it to
the creature's face. For a long time, they looked at each
other questioningly, until at last the other turned slowly
and began to paddle off yet further upstream, hungering
still for solitude and peace.

Ben drifted, floating with the tide. Several times he
tried to take up a handful of it, strange water; it fled
darkly out of his hand. Nor was it any the less strange for
being well-attested, or commonplace indeed, or indeed
the most familiar of the fluids. And as for the townspeople now turning fitfully in their beds, they were far too
accustomed to taking these phenomena too calmly—
such was his opinion of the Alabamians.

He returned before dawn. It was busy about the town
and yet he still had hopes of getting himself into his own
shop before anyone could notice. And that, of course,
was when he collided square into a big man in a suit, the
Supervisor himself who, apparently, had been waiting
there for some little while.

"No, sir," (he said), "*this* don't make any difference."
(He was fingering Ben's wet hat.) "You can swim all
night, if that's what you want. But come morning, and
you still got to *teach!*"

Nine

He was required to wait all the rest of that day and
much of the next one too, before a tall, raw, lantern-
jawed farm boy came in carrying a rooster in his arms.

Right away, Ben began to pack.

"Y'all got any . . . ?"

Ben nodded and then motioned him upstairs and into the split-bottom chair that sat in the corner.

"Oh, they'll pay you," said Ben, "the first of every month. See?" (He took out his bills, almost a hundred dollars' worth, and waved them slowly back and forth in front of the boy's nose.)

"Golly!"

"And this here's my commissioner's *Report*. Yes, I'm putting it right here, here where it'll be safe, here in my 'suitcase.' Oh, I know it's just a box. But I *call* it a suitcase."

"But . . ."

"Treat 'em right, the bees, and then they'll treat *you* right." (He hummed, throwing in the socks and underwear on top of the *Report*.)

"If you wern't in such an all-fired hurry . . ."

"Now if they *don't* pay you, shoot I'd quit, if I was you."

The day was bright and blue, many fat clouds washing back and forth in a sky that was large enough for even more. He hit the street at a gallop, whistling and singing his way to the courthouse where, even this early, some twenty rather exhausted-looking litigants had come out into the corridor, too tired to argue any further.

Quickly he slipped into the men's room, and then into the one vacant stall where immediately he began to vomit noisily. All around were farmers, each in a stall of his own—they stirred uneasily.

"That you, B. R.? I *thought* I recognized them boots."

B. R. said nothing.

"Aw, hell. They ain't nothing in this world but *kids*!"

B. R. puked again.

"They give you any trouble, just beat hell out of 'em!"

"Is that B. R. I hear? In stall number three?"

"Beat?"

"Shore!"

He backed out slowly, thinking on the man's words. It was the vastest building in the county, and from the window he could look out over the whole gorgeous countryside, a summer scene that ran all the way down past Wooley's shack, the broken altar, and edge of the earth. Would that he could go flying! Instead of having to stand up in front of a room of boys and girls who, very likely, knew more of spelling that he did himself. Indeed it was lovely this time of year, a calico quilt, as it were, made more lovely still through the cooperation of the farmers who had broken it down into squares, with corn here and beans there, cotton betimes and kudzu withal, hogs luxuriating in it.

"Better hurry, B. R."

He did hurry, the anger rising in him as he clopped down the hall, and rising still more when he remembered to come back for his box. He had *not* sprung forth into life in order to be disgraced in front of a class of rural churls who knew nothing of *his* knowledge, nothing of spelling, nothing of words, nothing of Haddenfield, and nothing of . . . Such was his frame of mind when he burst into the room with his face twitching and his good right arm already in position to come down heavily wherever it might be needed.

He found four boys, no more, and of these three of them were nervous and easily to be taught. It was the fourth boy doing the grinning, a large type, larger than Ben, with scars and marks and a shaven place on his skull where a wound was gradually healing. Of the girls, no one had said that one of them must be that same "Betty" who, could he have but seen her in her setting, was already higher at the waist than fennel, or nearly. He looked for, and did find, her little vial of colored ink—

she never went abroad without it. He could not bring himself to beat *her*, nor did the circumstances seem to require it. Suddenly, he yanked some spelling out of his pocket, but then pushed it back down again when he saw how the injured one was guffawing out loud at him (and smoking too), just as Ben had always foreseen that he would do.

His first impulse was to turn and go and come back no more, his second to step up straightway to the boy and come down hard on him with the book itself. For although he was a bad one, yet the crown of his head was highly pointed, and even fragile-looking, and had already a wound on it with stitching. Accordingly, the speller bent courteously, and courteously whispered in his ear. It was a big ear, clay in it, and much-bristled. B. R. could see his own message registering slowly in the other's eyes.

"I'll tear you up, boy, I sure will. Oh, I don't say it would be *easy*."

The boy thought, chewing more slowly now. Far away, a dog barked, the first to realize that soon enough winter would be coming in.

"How would you do it?"

Now was it Benjamin Reuben's turn to think. He was perhaps *too* conscious of the girl, her hundred acres, and in her hair the blue-green ribbon that so well sorted with the ink. Time was wasting. Finally he bent again, but instead of speaking, showed his own two hands, front and back, extending them at full expanse in front of the churl's vision. Those hands were hefty, and had some of the garden on them still; moreover, one of the fingers had been broken often enough that it produced a certain enough effect.

"That how you kilt that mule?"

Ben nodded. He had never meant to actually kill the thing.

"Well hell," said the boy, "I ain't got nothing against spelling. Pro-ceed, pro-ceed."

Ten

That day came when he owned above one hundred and thirty dollars—the result of the money that was handed out by the Supervisor himself (fresh green bills). Some, Ben spent. The better part, however, he hid, hiding it in the countryside itself during one of his late-night strolls.

On Tuesday, with the sun shining brightly, he stepped quietly into the crowd and began to move about the square. There was dignity in this, in the crowd, the sun, the square, and for a long time no one spoke. Hurriedly he skipped past the four Negroes, before the one with the glasses could remark about his new shoes.

It was on his third tour that he spotted the town's smaller lawyer (a napkin about his neck) eating with tremendous pleasure in the dark part of the town's best restaurant. Ben drew near, pressing at the glass. It looked to him more like breakfast the man was having, rather than any sort of proper lunch. He saw eggs, he saw bacon; indeed, he then saw the man lift his embroidered napkin daintily and proceed to blot his lips. Ben grinned and waved at him, whereon a shadow seemed to pass over the face of the lawyer, already in shadow. Finally, daubing and coughing and taking up his fork and putting it down, finally he summoned the speller to come and join him.

Ben ordered coffee, doing it jauntily. He had money and could easily afford such things as mere coffee, coffee served in a delicate white cup with the portrait on it of Washington and his wife.

"B. R."

"Howdy."

"The eggs, B. R., are good; I tell you this. Patsy alone knows how to prepare your true southern *egg*. Paprika on them! *That's* how she does it."

"Yes, sir. I knew they must be good, the way you . . ."

"You too, Ben; someday *you'll* want to know how to use a napkin too. See?"

Ben watched. The man also had a watch, its face also darkened, and with Roman numerals in place of outright numbers on it. Ben could not take his eyes off the watch, the band, the white cuffs and studs with their puzzling emblem of a snake crawling through the eye socket of a cow's gleaming skull.

"Don't be looking at that, Ben, while we're talking."

"Yes, sir."

"So! What did you want to talk about?" Suddenly, he looked at his watch. Such had been his education, he could translate the Roman numerals as quickly as if someone were whispering the information direct into his ear.

"I got me a job now," said Ben. "A real one."

"I heard that. I heard about it."

"Teacher."

"Yes!"

"And so . . ."

"And so you want *me* to tell you how to invest your money. Alright Ben, I could tell you how to place it."

"No, sir, I already placed it. That old bin down by Mitchell's field. No, sir; it's not money."

"Not money! That don't leave much to talk about, do it? You aren't looking for *spiritual* advice, are you now?" He chuckled, coughed, and then suddenly gathered up the last of the eggs, which had perhaps been over-fried, and let them dangle over his wide-stretched mouth. "Spiritual advice is free."

"Yes, sir. It's that gal over to the boarding house. Yes,

sir, I know she's skinny."

"I've heard. I've heard about it. They tell me you was holding hands with her too. Do you know what her mother is? Do you, Ben? No, let me put it this way: Do you know what her mother *used* to be?"

"Her mother is not any bit worse than my . . ."

"Alright, Ben. Sit, sit. What can *I* do? Patsy! You don't need a license to hold somebody's hand, you understand. *Now* where did she go? Patsy!"

"No, sir. I plan to marry her."

"Thought so."

"When she's fifteen."

"Wise, Ben; very wise. And you want *me* to do the marrying."

"No, sir."

"Hm? You ain't going to let Hubbard do it!"

"No, sir. We're going to Hermione."

"Jesus. You won't find nobody down there who even knows how to sign the goddamn document! Not in *that* town you won't." He ate. Then: "Ben?"

"Sir?"

"What do you want with me?"

"Well . . ."

"Hm?"

"Well I've never been married before, and . . ."

"Oh, oh."

"There's some things . . ."

"Oh Lordy! Jesus! Why me, Ben, *why*? Hubbard knows all about that sort of business. He's been married twice!"

"But he doesn't have any little boys and girls."

"Lots of 'em! Lots, Ben." Then, bending near: "It's his *wives* what never had the children. Patsy!"

Outside, a wagon rumbled past, its noise mixing with distant thunder. It never failed—each time he was entering upon a serious discussion, that was when great rains entered the town. The lawyer, meanwhile, had taken out a crush of papers from his vest pocket and, peeping now and again at Ben, was rifling through them wildly, quite indifferent, apparently, that one of the pages was lying in his plate.

"Rain," he said. "It never fails." He began humming.

"And she won't take off her clothes neither—she told me—not till she's *sixteen*."

"Lord, Lord, Lord!"

By early afternoon, the rain had come and gone, leaving all the various mules parked about the square in a refreshed and glossy mood. Patsy too had come and gone, absolutely refusing to fix breakfast fare at such an hour in the day. Itself, the room was nearly empty. But sometimes the manager, who seemed to fear the lawyer, sometimes he came to peep in upon them, always while wearing a smile. The lawyer himself had taken up the wrong end of the fork and was drawing with it in what was left of the grits.

"Ah yes," he said, "white womanhood. Treat them with respect, Ben, and don't fret too awful much over the family history. Now *here*"—he drew—"here you see those parts that must be treated with the greatest respect of all. You understand what I'm saying, boy?"

Ben nodded.

"They come to sharp points, two in number, and swell to various size. Now *here*, oh Lord right here, *here* is where the effluvium, rushing back, stirs up a veritable flux of the marital fluids, understand how I mean? That's where it gets touchy, Ben. One little tiny mistake and . . . Whew!"

Ben groaned. The man had not quite finished all the vitelline of the six eggs, with the result that some of the woman's upper body was melting quite away. All the lower body, Ben hardly dared look at it.

"Respect, Ben, respect. Respect it *here*, yes, and respect it *there* too."

"I do. And I respect *that* too."

"No, Ben, it's not necessary. *That* can take of itself."

"'Itself.'"

"Why yes. And you, Ben, can you manage your own . . . Your own 'here,' and your own 'there?' And bring forth many little goslings—will you, Ben?—each needing a lawyer of his, or her, own?"

Ben nodded.

"Good! And shall I show you how these goslings of yours, how they will be?"

He watched in fascination and alarm as the man pushed forward the salt and the pepper shakers, giving the speller a long, long time to look them over.

"This, then, is you. That's right! And this, Ben, this salt is *her*. Yes, and in a place like this, the salt probably is fifteen years old too. Now! watch carefully."

He did watch carefully. The lawyer had already opened the pepper and was pouring it with delicacy into the little porcelain pot-bellied salt dispenser that did in truth look to be somewhat pregnant.

"Mark me, Ben."

Ben marked. The man had replaced the lid and now was shaking the container vehemently with accompanying gestures, even while he went on staring into Ben with meaningfulness. And Ben continued to watch, even as the grains became increasingly, and indeed irretrievably intermixed, until it was one stuff, grey as the outside weather.

"Them's your children, Ben, all of 'em, right there in that little pot. Hear 'em wailing in there?"

Ben grinned. He was keeping the phial, putting it away in his pocket—the lawyer didn't care.

"That's right. It's a heavy responsibility, Ben."

"I know it."

"Heavy for *you*, with your father in you."

"My father is just as good as . . ."

"Better! Sit, Ben. It's not many men could build a tower two miles high."

"It's broken."

"So I've heard. And some of it's lying over in Pellene County, or so I've been made to understand."

"He's going to make it stronger next time."

By three, Ben felt he had acquired a far better understanding of children and women and their parts. The rain had come back, and the lawyer had opted to finished up his paperwork at the same table with Ben and the coffee and the woman in the grits. Finally, as four drew on, Ben rose up and paced over to the courthouse for his afternoon class. By five, he came back to find *both* lawyers, although at separate tables, and both refusing to look at one another.

"Will you join me, professor? For a bit of supper?" And then, bending over the table and hissing in Ben's ear: "No, no, no, don't look at him!" And then, speaking out loud and brightly, loud enough for Hubbard to hear: "Ah yes, it's a fine thing, literature. Tell me, professor—you can tell *me*—who *is* your favorite author?"

"Lippincott, I reckon."

"Ah! I don't know that one. You must tell me some day. Patsy!"

Eleven

Friday, he left town, moving without haste by way of the southern road until he came to Mildrew's gin. In front was unexplored terrain, green fields, and a corn patch so well-tended that each individual stalk seemed to be taunting at the sun with its tassels. Behind him the town lay under a fleet of clouds, or "galleons," (as they seemed to him), running away from battle—he could see

how distraught they were, the masts all broken off
among the tangled ropes. One ship indeed had dipped so
near the courthouse bell and steeple . . . But when he
looked again, the steeple was intact!

He went on, whistling. The day was simple, a few
twittering white moths following above and behind and
at a safe distance. He was at the top of his youth and his
strength, and he knew it. He strode past a field of cotton,
one single Negro plucking at it gingerly. Ben had learned
to endure the gang of crows that inhabited this part of
the county, and to accept more or less cheerfully—
nothing could be done about it—the sarcasms they
hurled down upon those who traveled by foot. Suddenly,
he broke out running, hoping to get out from under
them, but only then to slow again when he heard a wagon coming over the hill.

He traveled far, his extensive feet tearing up great
clots of ground. He was stronger, younger with each
step; let him grow any mightier than he was, any more
capable of larger draughts of the honeysuckled air, *then*
would he be too great for the world, and the world could
not abide him.

He gloated. What the crows did *not* know was that he
had some half-dozen good-sized pebbles in his second-
strongest hand. He had time, he could wait, waiting until
they swooped too low. Meanwhile, he focused his
thoughts upon those other forms, sixteen in all, that
were hiding themselves at various points in the woods
and fields. Thus he went on, smiling, pretending not to
see when he caught sight, here, of a weevil's tail, and
there a covey of trembling partridges.

Four miles out, he came to a tavern, a clay-made structure with a turfen roof and a fat woman sitting in the window with her legs hanging out. Ben tiptoed past, going on
for another twenty yards before she called him back.

"Hey, boy; I see you. Where're you headed with that—?"

"It's a suitcase." (He held it up for her to see.)

"Suitcase! That's nice."

Again he moved forward, again she called him back.

"Now what's he *got* in there, I wonder. Hey, boy!"

"Ma'am?"

"You got anything in there for me?"

Ben thought. The tavern, which might be full of people—he could see four tethered horses parked out back . . . He realized that he could not afford to begin passing out his possessions to anyone who asked.

"Well . . ."

"Yes?"

He pointed to the suitcase. "I've got my clothes in here."

"He's got his little clothes in there?"

"Yes, ma'am. And . . ."

"Hm?"

It was time to admit the truth. "And a dozen apples too."

"Ay, yi, yi! Apples! Okay, boy, I'll have me one of *those*. But you have to bring it to me."

Ben thought. In front, a low ridge of blue hills cut off all possibility of viewing any further of the undiscovered land that summoned him on toward Hermione. The earth, it seemed to him, was greater than he had realized, longer, fatter, sweeter, and, somewhere, with cities in it. And that was when the crows made their mistake. Ben hurled at them, catching them out of position at the very instant that he was himself at the top of his youth and strength. One fell, the most insolent of them, the whore watching with amazement as the bird thrashed about for a moment before expiring. The other birds flew away, woe streaming from every beak. Ben took one feather only, black and glossy, fixing it to his lapel.

He went on, mile after mile, deeper and deeper into a region of hyacinth and plum. His method was prudence itself; never once did he veer off into any of those manifold orchards so heavy-laden with exuberant peaches. And refused to take advantage when one of those same peaches actually hung out over the road itself, cooing at him. And cattle too—never had he seen such wealth, so many mirthful-looking calves dancing with such refined grace upon the carpeted heath. There was more to the world than he had known, a greater extent of forests, taller men, a higher grade of peaches. Once only he stopped, seating himself in an outburst of clover in order to study the procedures of the bees, big ones, yellow and gold, big yellow gold ones grown insane on the joys of hard work.

He passed the boundary at a little before two and then moved out across the narrow extrusion of the Ithomian County, a mere spit of territory, a quarter of a mile in thickness, predominated by pecan trees. Here, some fifteen Negroes had spread throughout the grove and were bringing in the nuts. Ben waved to the chief of them, a bitter-looking man who, apparently, had lost the ability to stand at full height. They looked at each other.

"You ain't got any business here."

"Going to Hermione."

"That right? Piss on it."

"Getting married."

"Piss on her."

"But I'm *from* Calauria."

"I had to kill a fellow from Calauria once. He even *looked* like you."

Ben nodded. "I got some brothers."

"Buried him down by the smokehouse. Plenty of room down there."

"I'm a teacher myself."

The man straightened up. "Never shot a teacher. What you got in that there little crate? I better not find any pecans in there!"

"No, sir! Apples."

"Piss on 'em."

The road narrowed, stopped. Ben had to go a full half-mile through a tract of pines, each pine deeply notched and throttled with a little collection cup for catching the precious sap—it made the whole forest redolent with his own favorite smell. Somewhere, no doubt about it, the juice was being rendered into turpentine; he could detect *its* peculiar whiff as well. It made him queasy, knowing that he was trending further and further from his own native grounds, deeper and deeper into pine and pecan barrens, further from home, closer to *her*, lost among peaches. He put on speed, singing to himself, unable to deny any longer that he was being trailed by crows in the sky whose cold silence was so much worse by far than their former yowling. Sun too—he was marching toward it at such an angle, the day might never end. He was extremely pleased therefore when the road picked up again, broader than before. It led, he knew, to Hermione.

His spirits improved even further when, toward three, he passed a succession of merchants who had come down to the highway itself, there to spread their tarpaulins and expose their goods. Ben saluted each of them with friendliness, pausing momentarily in front of the flute player with his jar of snakes. Ahead, a two-mule wagon was throwing up clouds of crimson dust that lingered a great while before settling finally over the leaves, the wrens, the merchants, and their wares. But all this was as nothing when compared to his surprise at finding a huge windmill that straddled the highway and allowed the traffic to pass between its legs.

It marked the end of the cultivated area. Ahead, he saw red waste, compacted earth in which not even so much as a cactus could be expected to grow. He entered therefore with real trepidation, regretting that he had not brought a supply of drinking water. As to the cause of all this aridity, the volcanos of Stymphalus County, he could still see the extinct cones lined up one after another in the extreme West, smoldering still. There, long ribbons of vapor trailed off to eternity, circumscribing the globe. He plodded on, shielding his eyes against the glare. A lizard ran across in front of him, but not *his* lizard. (His own lizard had ever been plump, even sedate, whereas this creature was a burnt-out case, with eyes that showed a trace of hysteria.)

At four, he passed a ruined farm, a splintered house, and a weather vane lodged upside down in the yard. The road bent now to the South, approaching, (but not touching), one of the former tributaries of the now altogether evaporated Cahawba stream. The crows had gone back; he looked for them in vain.

Thus it was close to sundown, at mile-marker twelve, when he arrived at last in a dusty place where three roads came together. One road, however, was but a mere path, and had that discontinuous quality of faint lines traced speculatively on old maps. (Oftentimes, these lines do not represent actual routes, no, but only rumors of them.) Ben plucked at his chin. Probably this fainter road led on to the village called "Helice," an unfortunate place long ago overthrown by earthquake and slides. Indeed, he thought that he could see an aura, a tragic one, hanging over the site in the afternoon heat. So intent was he, he did not at first mark the horseman riding up at a mad gallop from the other side. It was a wild-looking person, his hair flying out behind, his horse wild-looking too. Moreover, the pair was followed by a great black dog chasing along in their dusty wake. Ben waited upon them.

"Howdy!" he said. "Hot, ain't it?"

The man said nothing. Ben now observed for the first time the tiny shack from which, apparently, the man had issued. Unpainted, but with six brilliantly-colored banners furling in the breeze, it sat upon a little rising that overlooked the roads.

"*Real* hot."

The man dismounted and came toward him.

"Whew!" said Ben again. "Say, how far do you reckon it is to Hermione?"

"You ain't going to no Hermione, not unless you fight with me first. And *whup* me, I mean."

"Whup!" The man was red-headed, and had but one good eye. Truly, Ben was amazed; never had he put any credence in those old tales about the man "Cletus" and his methods.

"How come we have to fight? Naw, you're just *teasing* me. Ain't you?" He laughed out loud. The man, however, continued to take off his two shirts, to fold them neatly and put them away in his saddle bags. Ben judged him at forty, perhaps fifty years into his age.

"How come we have to fight? Say."

"How come some folks go clerking in dry goods stores? Hell, *I* don't know. You ready?"

"Wait! How come . . ." (Behind him, he knew, the highway led all the way back to town. He could still turn, if he dared, and walk home in perfect safety.) "How about if I just turn right around and go back in perfect safety?"

"Shore, you can do that. 'Course now, you can't expect me not to *tell* about it."

"I believe you would."

"Shore! 'He came, but would not stay to fight.' Is *that* what you want?"

"Wait! How about if I just go to Helice instead?"

"Helice my ass! There *is* no Helice, not anymore."

"Wait! You ought to know that I'm just about as strong today as I've ever been in my whole life. Look at me. And you, you're just an old man."

"Ready?"

Ben ran. He had chosen to make for the trees, there where the horse could not navigate. He had not counted upon the dog, a grand-sized affair with a head full of teeth and slobber. Now the monster was actually running out *ahead* of him, and smiling back.

"Shoo!" said Ben, kicking ineffectually at it. The man Cletus had needed a full six or seven seconds to get on horseback and turn the animal in the proper direction. It was too late—already Benjamin was in the trees.

Half an hour later and the speller found himself hobbling at speed through thistles and brush, always keeping a good slice of forest between himself and the highway. Sometimes there were bogs in his way, mosquito-laden, and sometimes sandy stretches in which nothing wanted to grow. As to the man Cletus, Ben could both *hear* him, (yowling up and down the road), and could *see* him, (great billows of dust), and never had so much anguish ever been heard in any single human voice.

Night did come. He had never had any gift for sleeping, and in any case he was so close now to Hermione that he could sense the near presence of it, as if God with his tremendous Finger was pointing to it from above. Itself, the evening was clear enough, and yet oddly, only three stars were anywhere to be seen. True, one star, the eye-destroying "Vega," had sagged so close to earth that he could have reached up and snatched it. Further, he could hear pigs feeding, and then the sound of a door slamming. For he was not so far from habitations but that the usual noises couldn't reach him. Here he sat, smoking, thinking, and brushing away ever and again the bothersome star.

It was well past midnight (Hermione no longer aglow) when he blundered all unknowingly into a Negro settlement and set off a crowd of highly indignant hounds who circled and threatened, but never actually came close enough to taste him. Of the Negroes, he found himself at once surrounded by them, old men for the most part, all of them with rifles. He saw women peering worriedly from the windows.

"Wal!" said Ben. "Shoot, I never reckoned *you all* were out here, minding your own business. Hot today, wern't it?"

"What you want?"

"Lord no," (said one of the women), "we ain't seen that boy for a *long* time! He never messed with her anyhow."

"Gone to California!"

"*She* started it, not him."

Ben, however, looked at them severely. "Now if I go *this* way, past that 'still,' now will *that* take me to Hermione?"

"He ain't in no Hermione, no suh!"

The dogs had gone off bored.

Exhaustion afflicted him. He computed that he had covered thirty miles already, even if some of it had been wasted space, owing to his detour. To go forward now, and then to wait around under her window for several hours waiting for the sun to come . . . It seemed bad policy to him. That was when he remembered that he had had no meals during the whole day.

He found a place, seated himself with dignity, and then opened the valise and took out two apples and a flitch of bacon wrapped in wax paper. His boiled peanuts had leaked, depositing a stain of brine. Never had he been more appreciative for such commonplace food. Finally he fell back, talking to himself, and then began pulling together a "blanket" comprised of leaves. He needed not many, the weather being kind.

He dreamt, and moreover knew himself to be dreaming. The dream itself? That the moon had not a man's face, but a woman's—that Cletus even now was bearing down on him—that he was being eaten by dogs—and then, toward dawn, that he had been given a list of words to spell, each word thirty miles long.

He was glad when it was morning. The birds descried it first, waking him with their prolonged discussion. He had seen his share of sunrises, he had *never* seen one like this—a narrow slit between two lids that held a most suspicious-looking eye; he jumped up at once.

He dined on nothing, preferring to make good time. It was his own favorite moment for walking; he felt he was trodding down the trees, a mile for every stride. *Here,* (here in the uplands), it was all clear day, whereas *there,* (there in the gulches), night still was dawdling on. He whistled shyly at first, but then soon broke out into unashamed singing. He passed under branches full of owls, all of them teetering perilously in their efforts to shake off the effects of last night's sleep. Ben hardly dared to look behind him, so much did he adore the sight of morning racing through the hills. In front, tendrils of smoke were climbing and tumbling and "falling" toward the clouds. This verified it—not *all* the volcanos were extinct.

It was mid-morning when he came into a tiny cemetery overgrown in kudzu and vines. He had no great distance to go, but now his excitement of yesterday was turning into a kind of fear. He simply could not recall precisely how the girl *looked*, even though, at the same time, he could hardly think of anything else. Strange business. Very soon now and he would be holding her, and doing it in a city that he had never in his life thought to visit. Moreover, on top of that, he knew there were scads of such cities, towns past numbering—they littered the South—and that in due time, if the strength availed him . . . And moreover, on top of *that*, that these same cities were getting huger every day. It dizzied him, the world; he wasn't sure yet he approved of it or not.

He napped for perhaps twenty minutes, and then rose and began to explore the graveyard. These were old inhumations, most of them; he saw one who had been laid to rest with nothing but a broken plowshare to mark the head and a pair of tiny shoes to show the feet. There was likely much treasure here—Ben knew the old-fashioned practice of burying specie and war medals along with the man. *He'd* not be the one to dig it up, never, nor send his soul to Hell. And that was when he saw a certain tombstone, or rather an oak plank that had been sawed to the size and shape of a tombstone. The inscription was faint:

O Lucy, if you should see me now!

Twice Ben read it, quite overcome by the horror of it. The buried man was not something he wanted to see, nor did he like to think that Lucy had seen it either. He wished too that these burials had taken place somewhat deeper than the three or four feet that were usual in those days. It was while he was backtracking that he saw the companion "stone," (also of oak); it lay some yards off. Perhaps the earth was softer there. Ben came forward, albeit reluctantly. It was about as he had feared:

Dear, be not ashamed.
For now I'm the same.

It was not until the late afternoon of the second day
that he came to the crest of a hill and was able to peep
down into the blighted Hermione, a dilapidated vale
spread over with a contamination of some sort that
seemed to rise from the river itself. And yet, the countryside that hemmed it in on three sides, it was as lovely as
any he had seen, dense with cattle, and crisscrossed with
creeks.

It was to be the sole time in his life when he was away
from Calauria. He knew, of course, that all these towns
sat by the same river, and drank from it; nevertheless, it
seemed to him that here the towns were even more unadvanced than upstream. It especially disappointed him
that they had chosen to build in this fashion, without
rhyme or reason, the houses all facing off indifferently in
whichever direction the carpenter happened to be standing at the time. And then too, he had heard reports of
how this place was riven by the three factions, called
"The Hill" and "The Field" and "The Harbor." Of "The
Field," Ben understood them to be the smallest party in
the town, also the most determined. Never yet, (so it was
said), had they tasted of power. He entered slowly therefore, his eye wide open for problems.

The streets, he saw, were not labeled. He could expect
neither a courthouse, nor Confederate monument, no
hotel, nothing of that sort in a town like this one. He
moved quickly, keeping a serious expression; the last he
wanted was to be noticed for what in fact he was—a
trespasser, a man with a suitcase, an upstream speller
having come with presents to fetch their best-looking
girl away.

He went first to the dry goods store, but then, finding
it poorly stocked and with hardly any organization to it,
he came out again and went across the road. He passed a
drunk man in galluses who, looking covetously at Ben's
valise, tried to rise from his chair and follow. Would

they, or would they not, the people of this town, identify his up-river accent? Finally, taking his courage, he went into the barber's shop. A farmer was having a shave, and next to him, a large man being treated for a gash.

"Howdy!" said Ben, (exposing his accent). "Couldn't tell me where I could find Miss . . ."—He gave the name of the girl—". . . could you?"

All four men turned and looked at him.

"What you want with her?"

"This fellow is not, repeat *not*, from around here," said the gashed man from under his towel and bandages.

"I just need to see her."

"From upstream, I'd say."

"Well you *can't* see her, not unless you got enough pro-visions in that there little briefcase of yours to git you all the way to Arkansas and back."

Ben grinned, but then did open the suitcase to show that he had but one remaining apple in it. The words about Arkansas, he viewed them as a joke.

"Your streets . . ."

"No labels!" They laughed.

"She lives over on *Reuben Kolb*—that's what she said. The last house."

"Yep, there's a last house there all right. But you won't find that skinny little gal there *now*; no, sir."

"What you want with that girl anyway?"

"Why, get married! We're getting married."

"I doubt it."

"'Married,' hell. Hell, that father of hers will tear you up, boy. You better git yourself on home, that's my recommendation."

Ben reeled, the town blackening in front of his eyes. He knew this, that the thirty miles he had traveled were as nothing when compared to the distance to Arkansas.

"Now how far is it, more or less I mean, to Arkansas?"

They tried not to laugh. The gashed man had arisen

and was putting on a dark blue suit that had a holster
sewn into the vest, and a revolver in the holster.

"Well," he said, "let me put it like this: you won't get
there on one apple."

"Better git you on home, boy—I'm telling you. Going
to be dark soon."

He drifted as in a dream, from one side of the town to
the other. The moments were passing, and soon it would
be dark in truth. He did identify the house at last, and
the very room that she had occupied—it had a curtain of
the exact cloth that matched her picnic dress. He
knocked twice, having to wait a great while before a fat
woman with two babies came and opened the door.

"I'm looking for . . ."

"Gone."

"Wait! My name is . . ." (He gave his name.)

"The speller?"

"That's it!" He jumped forward eagerly, absolutely certain that the girl would have left a letter for him, or a
memento at any rate, or something with clues telling
how to find her again.

"She left a letter. I'm supposed to give it to . . ."

"Me."

"Hold on! Now just hold on there, if you don't mind
too awful much, my 'good sir.' Now how do I know you're
the one, hm? Why, you could be one of those 'harbor'
people, for all I know."

"No, ma'am! I don't even like 'em, those people. No,
ma'am, I'm the one."

"Speller?"

"Yep. I mean 'yes.' That's me."

"I don't know."

"Yes, ma'am! Look at me."

"Alright speller, spell me . . ." (And here she gave the
girl's last name, a peculiar one deriving from the French.

Ben reeled.)

"I can spell her *first* name."

"Well I reckon so! *Anybody* could spell that. No, I'm sorry."

She started to close the door.

"Wait!" cried Ben. "Just wait. Now I can spell science words, lots of em! And I can . . ."

The door was shut. He saw too that an angry-looking man, entirely in tattoos, had come to the corner of the house, had ducked back, and now again was peering back at him. It dizzied Ben, this confusion of events; finally he called out, trying to maintain a tone of common civility:

"You can keep the letter—it's yours—but would you just *read* it to me please. Out loud? Once?"

No word. He divined that the woman had already retreated into the depths of the house and could hear him no longer.

"Harbor?" asked the man, still peering from behind the corner.

"No, sir! I'm not even from around here."

"That's worse."

"All I want is . . ."

"'Want'? 'Want'? Well what *I* want is for you to . . ."

"She doesn't even have to come outside!"

"That's right, she shore don't. And now that we're talking about it, what's that you got in that hand of yours, so scrunched-up? I don't like that, the way you're always hiding things."

"Ring!" He made hurry to open and show it to him, even taking it out of its little container and passing it over. The man looked at it astutely, turning it and even holding it up finally into the sputtering sun.

"I'll see she gets this, I sure will. She'll be real happy with it."

"Tell her to write me too."

"I will, I sure will. I'll do it."

"And tell her . . ."

"I will, sure will. And now you got about five minutes to catch that boat."

He wandered down to the wharf, head reeling, and then, without being fully aware of what he was doing, got aboard the night boat. It promised to be a sluggish voyage, moving against the current. Itself, the boat was heavy-laden and so cluttered with bales that Ben preferred to go forward and stand at the prow. Behind him, in his shack, the pilot was a timid little man, quite elderly, who appeared also to be ill; three times Ben saw him take out and drink from a little brown vial too tiny to contain spirits. In any case, the engine was noisy and didn't allow for conversation.

At three in the morning, they drove through a primitive settlement built on stilts where lights and lanterns gleamed along the shore. Here they slowed and went forward with circumspect. He was good at steering, the man at the wheel; nevertheless, Ben was somewhat taken aback when he bore toward the shallows and then handed off a toll to two men waiting in a skiff. Ahead were rapids; they passed over them easily however. It would be good sailing now—Ben expected no further troubles—good sailing all the way home.

Twelve

The weather turned gloomy, the days growing more and more disorganized as he himself spent longer and longer hours in his garden. Much of his time he spent in thinking about the past and its people, all of them now in paradise. And meanwhile, now, here, everywhere, there was this present generation, all soon to be in hell.

Once, when he was weeding at hazard, he heard a noise in the cabin. Ben groaned, believing it to be his neighbor's hound, an untrustworthy animal who had learned to open the door and to occupy the bed. This time however—and Ben jumped back in great shock—it proved to be his brother lying face-down under the sheets. Now once more, he wore a hood over his head, even as in the old days.

"Howdy!" said Ben.

"Got yourself a 'position'! How much they paying you?"

"I can't speak about that—it's a secret. Between me and the county. No, it has to be that way, Carl!"

"Goddamn, Goddamn it! I come *all this way*, thinking you might want to share. Now that's what papa would of wanted."

Ben hummed. It was true that he did have money, and true too that some of it was in the countryside and some in the bee skep, the last place on earth, (or so he liked to believe), where anyone would care to reach for it. "Shore wish I could help you, Carl."

"That's hooey. No, you're just too good for us now, I reckon, what with them . . ."

At once Ben took off his glasses and put them in his pocket.

". . . glasses. Did you know I haven't had nothing to drink for a *week*?"

"Week!" (He could see his brother's face now, a wasted terrain with one eye gone dead.)

"Don't be looking at that eye."

"But I could let you have some honey."

"No, I think father would have wanted me to have cash. Hey, what's all this I hear about you pestering some poor little old gal over in Hermione? Damn! Teaching her how to *spell*, is that what it is?" He laughed, a vile laugh that showed his teeth to be predominantly rotten, although with yet one good one in the front.

"It's dogwood honey. Shoot, you could probably trade it for some liquor."

They looked at each other.

"Alright."

Ben ran to get it, two earthen pots of a stuff so good and lovely that he hated to give it over.

"There! Well, good luck to you, Carl."

"I ain't left yet."

Ben hummed.

"Walking around at two o'clock in the morning, scaring folks. Shit, I don't know about you, boy!"

Now he left. Ben aided him to the street, aiding also with the pots and saddle bags. This was his sole brother to have come out his father's second wife, the one from Georgia. Accordingly, he had nothing with the others, save only the family limp. Ben waved to him, and then closed the door and locked the cabin and doused the lamp, and then lit the lamp, unlocked the cabin, opened the door, and tossed away the dog.

Years went by, or rather two months during which the weather deteriorated even further. It rained endlessly, so much so indeed that he must dash over to the courthouse during the intervals and then stand about in the hall until such time as class began. For he had left spelling behind, and now it was outright reading that he taught. And if as yet Calauria had but six educated men, still he was himself too young, too bashful too, to be put in seventh place. Therefore he still sometimes hankered back for the old days, before the planets had lapsed into their routes and every night the activity of volcanos promised a new surprise by morning, all of it long before the coming of the knowledge of spelling into the modern world.

He gardened by night, hoping in this way to take by stealth certain soil-thriving things that twisted and squirmed, and did indeed more often than not manage to escape between his fingers. He had taken to whoring too, having come to believe that it was the closest he would ever come to *holding* anyone, and the nearest to having anyone go on long walks with him.

Tonight, it was especially clear, a very great many bright stars visible. Himself, he was in his suit and moving slowly, armed with six roses from his own garden. At the corner, Mayfield's wife smiled and even nodded to him—she could have no slightest suspicion, of course, as to where he was going. Ben too, it was a mystery to him why he did the things that he did. (Unless he were even worse than he knew.) Two children strolled by, decent little people who were bound to find out someday what sort of human he had been. It was not too late to turn back.

The house was dim, a fewer number of candles than usual having been kindled; quickly Ben moved down into the further end, lest he be tempted to come flying out too early and end up having to spend the evening in his room. It was the evilest place in town. Some came for the liquor, some for the whores; Ben saw yet others who had come to do even worse than that, if only they knew what it was. One man had a knife, saying nothing. Of the whores, Ben preferred the old one, far more so than either of her daughters. He looked for her now, finding instead the man Abner seated at one of the tables. They nodded, whereupon the man climbed to his feet and came over to him.

"Benjamin Reuben."

"Howdy, Ab."

"Old Benjamin Reuben. I ain't seen you in so long . . . No, that ain't so; I seen you yesterday."

"I been teaching."

"If you want to call it that."

They glared. Abner too was a teacher, said to be a "teaching fool," he was so good at it. Nothing more troubled Ben than that the girl Betty attended Abner's lessons too.

"Hell," said Ben. "I did some teaching this afternoon."

"In Hermione?" He cackled. Ben had never liked this person—he was simply too large and too coarse, and had a carbuncle situated precisely between his two overheated eyes that blinked so seldom, or never. "And now," he went on, "I reckon you figure on getting into Hattie again."

"I might."

"Might not, too. She's bleeding."

Ben stood, but then sank back down again.

"Bleeding!" said Abner. "I tell you, it happens every goddamn time I get paid!"

(A wild thought had come to Ben, namely that the woman might now be willing to go for a walk with him.) He said:

"Well. Reckon I'll take my leave, as the poet says."

"Hold it! That's another thing—I don't think you ought to be teaching Betty any more of that *reading*, and so forth. D'you hear?"

"Why, she's the best reader I got."

"She don't need that! Anyhow, you wouldn't know what to do with all them acres anyhow."

"I reckon I would."

"Shit, you couldn't even make a crop, not like me, not even if cotton was a dollar a pound."

But B. R. had no intention of getting into a brawl with this man who, in any case, was largely drunk by now. He said:

"It's a wonder to me, how anybody that teaches *figuring*, how they can't do any better when it comes to knowing whether a person is going to be bleeding or not."

The man half-stood. *"You're* here."

"Never said I was no mathematics expert."

"No, nobody could say that."

"Nobody. No, what we need in this county is good-spelling people, not just more damn old ciphering, we don't need that."

The man now rose three-quarters of the way. Having started, Ben could not bring himself to stop.

"That's right, Ab, the *quadrivium*—I've read about these things. Spelling, reading. Now you take Dickens, now that's what we need in this county."

"Dic . . . ! Why you damn fool, Dickens is dead!"

The man was laughing again. Looking at him, Ben could distinctly see that his teeth were generally of gold, a metal that he was ever after to associate with a facility for numbers. At the same time, he recognized that the farmers were crowding around, hoping still, just as they had been hoping for years, hoping for a fight between these two at last.

"Dickens! Whee!"

Of the daughters, the pale one had come out in her slip and was laughing too. Ben lurched for his hat, found it, and then strode to the door. It was a sorry group of people. And yet, he found that he was still reluctant to depart and to have to trod back to his quarters, knowing, as he did, that he had already many times over read all the material that was there. Nevertheless, he now did pull open the door, and go outside in dignity.

He had put his hat on wrongly. It was cold weather, by Calaurian measure; strangely, his thoughts were upon the *Agricultural Colleges* essay (by Henry French) in his commissioner's report. No sleep tonight!

Within minutes, he found himself at the edge of town and gazing north. He wished now that he had had far far

more to drink than he had had—the scene was bleak, the
moon peakèd and pointèd, the wolves presumably lean.
The North looked flat to him, with myriads of cannon
and grinning troops. Yes, it would be on just such a night
as this one, when they were most likely to reappear.
Eastward, of course, were the dried-up civilizations,
Chaldeans and the like who had done well enough (up to
a certain point), working with clay.

Better that he too had come forth in some previous
Age, instead of here among mules and whores, grist mills
and cumbersomeness. His own face, it too was so much
like a horse's, so long and far away that he had to reach
out a full length to tap its various points. Next, he covered himself in his scarf, a habit like his brothers'. A
woman came by, a pretty one, someone's wife; in spite of
his better self, Ben followed. Always he had wanted to go
out walking with someone of this very sort; instead, one
block further, she turned and entered the second-best
house in town.

He was the last man in the county still to be awake at
this hour. However, where there was thought, thought
unto print and print upon the page . . . The lamp sput-
tered, and with it the horror that he might be left in the
dark with all the Commissioner's wisdom wasting in his
arms. He did *want* to sleep. Finally, toward three, he lifted the mantle and blew out the flame.

Thus Ben: at three-thirty, he found himself deep beneath the covers, still tapping quietly at various places on
his long, far-away and very wooden "face-like-a-horse's."

Thirteen

When after a day of classes, oftentimes he would
wander back to his room and sit for certain hours think-

ing of nothing, or of the girl, or of the past. And in all that time, until he was twenty-six, he received but one further letter, a short message in a trembling hand telling how his lizard, deteriorating by the hour, had gone down to the Edge one night, (starry night), and not come back.

There came further days and further nights, Ben keeping a close count upon them until the lizard rose again (rising in armor newly-burnished), as six bright stars in the North-northwest. Accordingly, he did not at first give much heed to the fire that had broken out in the western hills, a minor blaze—so he thought—until suddenly it flared up higher than the trees. Truth was, he had grown somewhat blasé about these nightly conflagrations, the great destruction of the farmers' homes, most of it due to lightning strike, or to the new vogue for electricity and its things. Again, he went to the window. Yellow fire—it meant pine. However, *this* fire seemed situated in the precise same spot as Betty's house.

He ran forth, but then had immediately to come back for his shoes. For a long time now he had been wanting to distinguish himself in front of the Calaurians. Certainly no one could run faster than he. He passed the courthouse, the site of this morning's unsuccessful lesson, and then next the feed store where some half-dozen deliriously happy old men had gotten to their feet and were exclaiming and pointing to the blaze.

"There goes B. R.!"

Ben put on speed. He had been hoping to distinguish himself in front of the Calaurians, wherefore he needed a world of fires and near-drownings, Northern invasions, anything and all things except another twenty-seven years like these last ones. Now the tocsin could be heard from all the denominations, but especially from the *Last Chance Baptists* whose giant zinc bell, the largest in the town, was tolling lugubriously indeed.

Ben went faster. He could not expect to catch up with the men on horses, nor with the two or three wagons that had such a start on him. As to the girl Betty, he had a clear premonition of her standing out in her field, the same sloppy blue ribbon in her hair, still wringing her hands in the same way as when she couldn't spell a word.

He turned in at the lane and then sprinted down past a gathering of anxious-looking farm wives who took no joy in the destruction of a home. The girl . . . Ben saw first the ribbon. However, he had come for combating fires, not for standing about commiserating with a mediocre speller who now was jumping up and down in high dismay.

Three times he went into it, bringing out a lamp, a harness, an assortment of bedding, and, (and this was the best deed available to him), salvaging the cat. It was on his fourth trip that he brushed into Abner. They stood, facing one another in extreme calm and, even though the roof might fall in upon them at any moment, in boredom even.

"Ab."

"B. R."

"Good rain, we had yesterday."

"We needed it."

"Need it now!"

They laughed. Finally:

"No need for you to piddle around here, B. R.—*we* can finish up, me and the boys."

"Them 'boys' don't seem too interested, not in coming in *here*."

"Probably afraid of that roof."

"Probably."

They looked up at it. The joists were hefty enough, or had been so at one time. Now they hung by a thread.

"I found the cat."

"I seen you. But *I'm* the one what saved the kittens."

"Did you *count* them, Ab? And did it *add* up right?"

"I tell you the squat truth, Ben, why don't you just run on back to your goddamn little hole-in-the-wall, the one with the dog-in-the-bed, you hear?"

"No. No, I don't think so. No, she's going to need some . . ."

"She don't need nothing of yours!"

"And where're your *shoes*, Ab? *I* got shoes."

Two beams then fell; it opened up a space in the roof through which Ben could see a part of the enormous constellation called "The Lizard," including the whole shoulders, neck, and smiling face. Another minute and the house would be gone, vanished into sparks, nor could he understand how the ruffian in front of him was able to endure doing without shoes, not in circumstances as hot as these. Himself, with the heat at his back, he wanted to die and be done with it.

"Going to rain tomorrow too—that's what they say."

"Good for the crops. Goddamn you, B. R.!".

They looked, looking at the ceiling and then at each other, and then both of them dashing outside together to check on the barn. Was it too in flames? That was when for the first time Ben laid eyes upon the girl's father, or grandfather possibly, a wild-looking galoot in overalls who was dancing about the house in exultation.

Now at last, the flames took on a spiral shape—Ben knew what that portended—and commenced to groan in a way that meant the fire was nearly over. The girl, meanwhile, was clinging to the farmer next to her, a forty-acre man whose own career had been none too lucky. Ben went to her. Outside of class, they had never until now exchanged a single word of conversation.

"Ah well," (said the speller), "it's almost over." Then: "I saved the cat, and the kittens are fine too."

"We have no place to live in!"

"I know it. It's deleterious. However, you do have all

this land."

"Oh."

"And so let's go and look at it, you want to?"

He had never touched her before. The forty-acre man used the chance to get away. Ben conducted her, nudging her forward past the Calaurians, past the barn, (which remained intact), and thence to the meadow that lay over against Glen Mitchell's place. It was a pity this patch had not been better tended—he saw everywhere feathered thistles crowding out the grass.

"And nothing to wear!"

"You're wearing something now."

That was true. The crowd had gone off, but then had come running back when at last the roof did collapse in upon itself, sending up a bright green plethora of gorgeous sparks; they swooned at it. It gave a momentary view of the interior, and of the stodgy black stove to which the fire could do harm at all.

"See? And you've still got a stove too."

She had to admit it.

"So let's us just go down here a minute, you want to?"

Such was his mood. Also, he could catch glimpses of Abner dashing this way and that, hunting for the girl. Himself, he had not thought of going in unto the girl, although she was old enough, and though it might distinguish him in front of the Calaurians. Rather, he wanted to go for a walk with her while he was in this state, and while the moon too was as *it* was.

"Look at that moon!" (Smoke passing over the face of it.)

No, she continued to look back ruefully at what had been her house. Her father meanwhile, or grandfather, appeared highly disappointed that the people were leaving, and so early in the evening too. Ben turned to the girl. They were strolling downhill, into regions that he had only been able to guess at, those times he used to pass by on the highway. Here, the gradient was by no means so severe that corn could not be grown, yea even cotton as well. Ben now counted the acres, all of them fallow and, in the moon, all of them loamy to a degree.

"Mellow!" he said. "Yes, and friable too, from the looks of it." He had to drag her, as it were, even while he stepped off the measure. He spied a plow, an antique one left precisely where someone, eons ago, had run off and left it. Other than for that, he felt he was moving out over a surface where no white man had ever yet stood.

"Lord, Lord. Now how many acres do you have here exactly?"

She looked back toward the house. "We used to have a section," she said, still wringing her hands. "But not anymore, oh no. Jasper, he sold some of it. And didn't even tell me!"

"The rascal. But how much is left?"

She told him, and the number she gave was the number that he had heard before. Now, finally, at last, after these years, the truth fell down upon him in amazing clarity.

"Why . . . Good Lord, you need a husband!"

She was taller than the fennel, or nearly. Still, she wouldn't look at him. No one else had come to as many classes, week after week, learning no more than she had.

"Why, yes!"

She was old enough. Meanwhile, to the South, there was open land, some of it waste. His mind ranged over the possibilities of orchards, of grazing, of pollen for the bees, and even, (and he had taken this from books), of goats for the milk.

"This is thin, this."

She blushed.

"But friable. *We* could make something of it."

She brightened. More worrisome to Ben were the landcrabs, a whole nation of them set into irritable movement by the blaze.

"Sheep too, maybe."

She smiled. He divined that she might have a vocation for animals, hoofed ones, and that all-in-all she'd make a fine wife.

"You'll have to do as I say, of course—I want that understood at the start. The children too. Tell me, does that boundary go *all* the way to that fence line there? Lord, Lord!"

It was lush pasturage, even up to the knees. Seeing that it was so deep, and that the girl was as yet dizzy from this evening, he lifted her easily and continued to measure the distance while she gazed skyward in his arms. Ahead, he saw a grove of pine, the trees standing so close together that he had trouble finding a way inside.

She was lusher than he knew. *Now* was he appreciative for what he had learned from others, applying it with confidence to *this* one, even while this one had still the fire in her thoughts and . . . he knew not whatall in her eye.

Fourteen

They married, him her and she him. Memnon came, also Benjamin's father who walked all around the girl three times, estimating the years and the sum of work that one might rightly expect to have from a person of her type and structure. But in truth, the old man tired easily, and had not been the same since his tower had broken off in high winds, leaving the best of it in someone else's field.

Ben drove her home through cheering crowds. In fact, the weather that day was awful, and instead of crowds, they had to whip the mules through four miles of a dense grey rain that drenched the wife, destroyed the cake, made a puddle in the buggy, and caused the mules to stink. And where *now* were the dry goods of yesterday? And that was when he saw Jasper lying outside in one of the puddles, happy but drunk. For one brief moment, Ben's optimism almost failed him. Great clouds were forming in the West, and behind that, the likelihood of drought and storm, of hurricanes, insect-infestation, and many other possibilities besides. He wanted to weep, and might have done so, had not his bride already been weeping for the past half-hour.

There among alien dogs, he tried now to count his assets. He had given away his academic position and never again was he to be called "speller," or "professor," or any of the other names he so enjoyed listening to. Clearly, his assets were few. And when he turned to speak . . . Never before had he had a "bride" at his side.

"Boy howdy, you look funny. What with that 'veil,' I mean. It's good for the crops though, I reckon. Rain."

"We don't have any crops!"

"We will, we will. Shoot, someday . . . Hey! What you crying for?"

"And no place to live in!"

"Got the *barn*, don't we? Shoot yes we do." Then: "Your grandaddy's about to drown."

Ben rushed to him. Or rather, tried to do so. For that was when the dogs, sensing his discouragement, at last delivered their attack.

That first night, he lay with his wife, side by side. The yellow moon continued to be plump, and sent long fingers into the loft that allowed him to look into her face and search behind her ear.

"Here it's dry," he said. Then: "Now don't you worry! I'll bury them tomorrow."

"They used to be good, when they was just puppies."

"Say, what are you wearing, I wonder? Under that

sheet?" He put his hand out toward her, she pushed it back. In the light, he could not rightly say which girl she was, whether from Hermione, or whether Hattie's younger or whether elder daughter. Not Belinda, he no longer expected *that.* Then: "Hey! You still got your stockings on!"

"Hush."

It was a most imperfect roof; smoking quietly, he could see directly into the sky where "The Mule" was heading down, nose first, into a smattering of very bright stars somewhat to the east of "The Crab." Soon enough, they would join in their bloody fight that took place each night during this time of year.

"I'm going to put that forty into corn," he said. "What with cotton at eight cents. I don't see we got much choice."

His bride said nothing. It was her way, apparently, to lie flat on her stomach, making it nigh impossible to touch her critical parts. Ben came nearer. "Corn," he reiterated.

"The Mitchells, they'll help shuck. We used to help them."

"Yes! And Grady—I owe him a whole bunch of dimes."

"Hens."

"Yes! That will be for *you* to do. *Red* hens?"

She nodded with enthusiasm made new. "I used to tend thirty of them, near about. More!"

"You never had no thirty!" said Jasper.

Ben came nearer. He had been able to worm his hand into the straw, and then to come up *under* her. Lying now on her back, one of the beams had elected to smite into her wide-stretched eye, the one closest to Ben. He counted, waiting for that moment when "The Mule" and "The Crab" came together at last, and being witness to it when she saw what followed, and seeing how the horror of it registered in her eye.

It needed nine full weeks to turn the barn into a home, and two weeks beyond that to make a barn. All these projects, barn, new fencing, two cows, he took all into his own hands. Jasper too he took, commanding him to this and to that, and supporting those commands with hard looks that the man could not endure. The woman he did *not* command; right away, she assigned herself to the hens, the garden and vines, her flower patch, the two cows. Vast was her bonnet, huge, blue as the flowers, and the woman within it small, brown, smiling. Of the dogs, he slew two more of them, and the rest obeyed.

One day, he was out digging a "root cellar"—his government bulletin had recommended it—when Abner came driving up. Ben was displeased to see how he came on straight across the field itself, destroying the tender corn beneath the wheels of his smoldering automobile. On the other hand, Ben was pleased to see that Jasper had immediately gone for the shotgun. Betty saw none of what followed—her bonnet was too large, and she herself too engrossed in the chickens. Himself, Ben bent to his task, taking out another spade full of soil. The red clay earth of Alabama! The stuff was notorious for holding capacity, wherefore Ben found that he was shoveling almost as much water as of clay. All day the sun had been warm, pleasant, helpful; now, however, Abner was standing in the way.

"What in the . . . !"

"Root cellar."

"Root? Why you damn fool! You figure this here's *Iowa*, do you?"

Ben had to laugh. "It's not just roots, Ab, no. No, it's tornadoes too, you understand."

They looked at each other. The man was tall, taller than Ben, and large, more so than nearly anyone Ben knew. As for the speller, the better part of *him* was in the hole.

"You took the girl too. Didn't you?"

"I did."

"Why, I been teaching her for lots longer than *you*! Now is that true, or ain't it?"

Ben acknowledged that it was.

"Well tell me this—how much is it? Is it 200?"

"No, no; oh no. Less! *Much* less."

"Is it 150?"

"Nineteen is waste."

"Waste, hell. You'll find something to do with it, I'm sure of that."

"Not if you elect to kill me. With that knife of yours."

"I ain't going to *kill* you exactly. I just want to . . ."

Ben hummed.

"And so if you'll just kindly climb out of that hole—you going to?"

The speller thought about it. He knew, as Abner did not, that there was an old man on the porch with a shotgun in his arms. Ben now scooped up a full shovel of water and earth, red gore as it looked, and unloaded it on top of the polished toe of the man's mint-new boots.

"I see. You take the land, you take the girl."

"I do."

"And now you're dumping that stuff all over my new shoes."

"Yes." He did it again. Jasper, he saw, had arisen, but then had gone back inside. That was when Abner leapt into the pit.

Thinking back upon it later, Ben was grateful that the space had been as constricted as it was. The man had massive fists to be sure, but very little room in which to give momentum to them—Ben saw right away that he could absorb a number of such blows, provided that he remained curled up in his fashion. And then too, he was aided by his last remaining dog, the best of his whole litter, who went especially for the man's new shoes.

"Whew!" said Ben, having taken a hit to the eye. "You shore know how to hit a fellow!"

The rooster too was now embroiled with them, having fallen into it by accident. Ben rose up quickly and then ducked back down again—it allowed him to verify that Jasper had come back out to the porch and was rocking serenely in his chair. Abner slowed, and then stopped.

"That's twenty. Want more?"

"Twenty-*two*," said Ben. "No, no."

"You got blood all over you, B. R. You better see to that."

"I plan to."

"'Cause otherwise . . ."

"I know it."

"Your nose is broke too."

Ben agreed. "Now if you'd stopped at twenty, why then it wouldn't be broke."

"I know you got more than 150, B. R.; I know it."

"Shore! If you include the waste."

"There ain't no 'waste'!"

Ben now gathered himself in the bottom of the hole, using his murdered dog to absorb some of the kicks. That was when he received a terrific pain, well-aimed indeed, that went right to the spleen. Those new shoes, they had blood, they had clay, they had a number of tooth marks too.

Fifteen

The courthouse had a room on the third floor, and in that room there was a government man who remained all day behind a desk crowded with potted plants that represented one or another of the viable southern crops. For a long while, Ben remained in the hallway, until the man chanced to glance up from his work.

"Christ!"

"Howdy."

"Good God in heaven! Did Cletus do this? It's your *nose*, Ben; it's bleeding over all your shirt."

Ben sought frantically for his handkerchief, a great square thing that the manufacturer had been wise enough to cut from red cloth. But mostly it was the region beneath the ribs on the right side, there where Abner had scored the best by far of all his blows.

"Tsk, tsk, tsk," said the agent. "Primitive, very primitive. I look at you, Ben, and I see a nose bent over to one side. I see two bad eyes too."

"Yes, sir. It's bad here too." (He pointed to that place.)

"Awful, just awful. No, don't worry about that carpet. Too late anyway. Well! Good rain we had, what?" Suddenly, he leapt up and then sat again. Never had Ben known so nervous a type.

"Yes, sir; I reckon."

"Yes. Actually, I've been waiting for you to stop by, waiting for quite some little while, if I may say so. Come into some *land*, have we?"

"Yes, sir. Near about a hundred acres of it."

"One hundred and eighty, actually."

"Nineteen is waste."

"No Ben, there *is* no waste, not with land. Not when you know how to cope with it."

"Put a few peach trees on it, I reckon."

"No, Ben; I won't hear of any more peaches, not unless you plan to feed 'em to your hogs. Besides! They got all that . . ." (And here he made an expression of nausea.) ". . . all that goddamn hair and fuzz *all over* 'em!"

"I don't got any hogs."

"Get some! Today!" (He stood, and then sat again.) "I mean it, Ben."

"Yes, sir. I got some new fencing up already."

"Now you're talking. You must never let any of those

things, hogs, wander about at freedom, Ben."

"No, sir."

"Filth, pure filth, all filth. You ever done a study of those things, Ben? You wouldn't never guess this was a Christian county."

"No, sir."

"Lambs now—your lamb is just . . . nicer. Get lambs, Ben."

Ben thought. "I *could*, I reckon."

"Absolutely. 'Course now, you don't want 'em in your garden."

"Oh no."

"No scruples, Ben; they'll eat your goddamn house, your horse, your wife, every goddamn thing you got! I had me a sheep one time. The smell! And then of course he had those *testicles*, like they do. Dragging on the ground. Goats are different."

"Yes, sir. Now about corn . . ."

"Indigo! keep away from it, Ben. There hasn't been any indigo in this county since the Confederacy. It stains your hands too."

"Yes, sir. I . . ."

"See this?" (He pushed forward one of the potted plants which, also, he had been using for a spittoon apparently.) "This here's what you want. This here's the future you're looking at, Ben, right here; see it? Goddamn little yellow blooms?"

"Yes, sir."

"That's *money*, Ben, *real* money. You sew forty acres to *that*, you got money coming out your ears."

Ben grabbed for his ear, the one that Abner had so thoroughly boxed. "Yes, sir. What is it?"

"What is it? Lord, I'm supposed to know *everything*, is that how it is? On *my* salary?"

"I been thinking about cotton."

"Cotton is eight cents. Why Lord, you can't make

enough on cotton to . . . Hogs can't eat it. Dogs can't. *You* ever tried to eat it?"

"No, sir."

"Then you can't expect them to eat it either, can you?"

"Reckon not."

"No." Suddenly he began scratching violently, a spasmodic event followed up by prolonged sneezing. His potted specimens, some of them appeared not to agree with him.

"Corn . . ."

"Keep away from it, Ben. Too high."

"Seed cost too high?"

"Seed hell, it's the goddamn corn that's too high! Can't *see* anything, with all that . . . I call 'em 'weeds.' All that growth, and everything." Then: "You ever been to Birmingham, Ben?"

"No, sir."

"Now *that's* the way to do it—no hogs, no corn. You stand there, Ben, in one of them 'intersections,' (they call it), and you can see for miles and miles, no hogs, nothing like that." (He had on a paradisiacal expression.) "And then at night, you come home and your boots are just as clean as they were that morning!"

"Whew!"

"They've got *places* there, Ben."

"I've heard about it."

"*Bad* places." Suddenly, he jumped up and began scratching fore and aft about both knees. "You wouldn't even want to hear about those places, Ben. Would you?"

"Cows now, what . . . ?"

"Keep away from 'em, Ben."

"Too big?"

"Too big? Jesus. Big is what you want! No, no, no; not too big. Too *many*."

"'Too many.'"

"Why certainly. I don't know if you've ever given this

any thought, Ben, but . . ."

"No, sir."

". . . but just imagine there was as many cows as there are . . ."

"Acorns?"

The man stopped, sat, and then looked back at him coldly. "'Acorns,' did you say? I never thought you'd do that, Ben—come up here to make fun of me."

"No, sir!"

"'Acorns.' Now just how in hell could there be as many cows as acorns, hm? It doesn't stand to reason, Ben. So why say it?"

Ben looked down.

"Why Lord, we wouldn't have room to turn around! No, no; keep away from 'em, Ben, cows and acorns."

The bank was just across the square. Ben hastened to it, hoping to find that Seth had not already gone off to the *Last Chance Tabernacle* for mid-day services. It surprised him to find that here too, in the most luxuriant office in town, even here two potted plants of the new kind were being cultivated in empty coffee cans, and that one of them was already producing a fruit that looked like beans. The man himself was in his office, dressed in a tie that bore the emblem on it of a bleached cow's skull with a snake emerging from one of the eye sockets.

"Benjamin Reuben! How does it feel?"

Ben grinned.

"One hundred and eighty acres! Congratulations, my friend."

"It feels pretty good."

"But those *eyes*, and that *nose*! That *doesn't* feel so good—am I right?" He laughed merrily. He had a plush chair in green leather, and so cleverly put together that the man could twirl about in a full circle, had he wanted to do it. "How much you looking to borrow, B. R.?"

"About three hundred dollars. Or shoot, I could make do with just *two* hundred."

"Two hundred. Hell, Ben, you got that much already. Buried in various places. How about all those silver dollars you hid on McCleary's place?"

"No, sir; somebody took those."

The man sighed deeply. "But Ben! How about Betty's daddy? Or grandaddy—*he* must have all kinds of money by now."

Ben took it out, many hundreds in Confederate currency which, however, no longer enjoyed any credence in the county. Seeing it, the banker began to laugh.

"Now you hold on to that, Ben; that's good stuff."

"Yes, sir."

"Because someday . . . Someday, someday, someday. Oh, I don't say that *I'll* live to see it; I'll be gone by then. But not you Ben, not you."

Ben came nearer.

"Oh Ben, the things that you will see. Ohio, New York. That old flag of ours flying over New York?"

"Or just one hundred—I could get by on that."

"Canada! *They* don't know what to do with it. But we would, wouldn't we, Ben? And that's not just 180 acres we're talking about neither."

"It's more."

"So I want you to save that stuff, Ben, save it. No! don't tell me where you're putting it. Let it be a secret between you and . . . And don't stick in there with your bees neither."

"No, sir. Shoot, I could probably get by on seventy-five dollars, if I had to."

"Seventy-five green American dollars," said the man, repeating it as if in a dream. "Ah. But you see, Ben, you don't have any experience as a farmer. No 'proven record,' as we say. Understand? Now if it was *spelling* . . ." He laughed merrily. "Cotton is eight cents."

"Yes, sir. Shore could use that money."

"I know you could. I know it. You need it real bad too, don't you?"

"Yes, sir."

"Well that's the worst time to try to get it, Ben, when you need it."

"But . . ."

The man held up his hand to stop him. "Come back, Ben, when you *don't* need it." He laughed happily. "Will you?"

"But . . ."

"It's like *me*, for example. I can borrow all the money I want—did you know that?—and I don't even need it."

"But . . ."

"Yes, it's a strange and marvelous system, Ben. The better it gets, why then it just gets better. And it gets *easier* too, the better it gets. I don't know why."

"But if it gets *worse* . . ."

"Oh Ben. Don't even talk about it. But you're right— the worser it gets, why then the harder it is to keep it from getting worse."

Ben thought. "Now if a fellow had a thousand dollars..."

"Yes?"

"And he wants another hundred dollars . . ."

"That's easy."

"But if he's only got *one* dollar . . ."

"Hard, Ben, that's hard. In fact, I wouldn't even be talking to a fellow like that."

Ben thought, plucking at his chin. "Now if a fellow had a *million* dollars . . ."

"Why then, when he wakes up, why he'll find that he's a hundred dollars richer than when he went to bed! That's the genius of it. See? You'd think it would be the other way around, wouldn't you?"

"But it ain't!"

They laughed both, both overcome by the hilarity of

it. Ben stood and shook with him cordially—they
laughed again—and then, listing somewhat in the dense
nap of the carpet, tiptoed from the room.

There was in those days a general-purpose store that
sat close by to where Wooley lived; Ben entered it now,
aware that everyone had fallen silent when they saw
what condition he was in. It was his favorite place in the
world, owing to the good management and to the quantity of things set out on shelves that reached from floor
to ceiling. Today, a Negro in overalls was feasting at the
oyster bar and had devoured so many of the things that
he had built up a hill of shells that wouldn't allow Ben to
see his true identity.

"Howdy," said Ben, addressing himself to the proprie-
tor.

"Yes, sir; I've got just what you need, Ben. Just smear
it on your face and . . ."

"It don't hurt. *Here's* where it hurts." (He pointed to
that place where, as he supposed, his liver was pinched
between two ribs.)

"I can't help you there, Ben. You ought to see somebody."

Ben nodded. "I saw Seth."

"Seth!"

The Negro had stopped eating and, his head inclined
to one side, seemed to be listening with great attention.
Ben spoke up loud and clear.

"Need to borrow two hundred dollars, Claude; I sure
do."

There was a silence throughout the store. The Negro
ducked down behind his shells.

"Two?"

"I sure do."

"Cotton is eight cents this year, Ben."

"I know it. I'm thinking about corn."

"Corn spoils, Ben. Cotton, it don't never spoil."

"I know it. But cotton is just eight cents this year."

They looked at each other over the counter. He was a decent man, the store owner, but so full of gains and losses and troubles, so many jars and boxes and so much sweeping to be done that his apron had turned black from it and his face wore a permanently anguished look. Also, he had two coils of gummed paper dangling from the ceiling, each bejeweled with fly corpses, and other things as well.

"Two hundred dollars."

"Yes, sir."

"And what if we don't get any rain?"

Ben thought deeply.

"How will you pay me back?"

"Maybe I could borrow it from Seth."

"'Seth.' Seth don't lend money to poor people, I thought you knew that."

"Then I'll pay you back *next* year."

"We'll all be old men by then, Ben. For example, take Willie here." (The Negro ducked deeper behind his shells.) "Willie here, he already owes me *more than three hundred dollars*. Ain't that right, Willie? And Willie's a nigger!"

"Shore! But Willie's got sons. Three of 'em."

"Those sons aren't any good! I thought you knew that. Are they, Willie? Besides, two of 'em are in Birmingham."

Ben sighed. By the register, there was a glass case dedicated, in part, to bags of boiled peanuts, and in other part to a display of some of the major curiosities of the county—arrowheads mostly, but also an enormous hen's egg that had started out to be twins. Ben could not look at it without thinking upon the misery of the hen that had brought forth such a thing.

"Two hundred dollars."

"Yes, sir."

"There'll be some interest, Ben."

"Maybe I could borrow that too."

It was the most famous cash register in town, and known to a much wider circle than Seth's foot-thick vault. Ben watched (Willie rising too) as the drawer came open to the sound of bells, revealing any number of neatly-stacked American green bills sorted into little oblong compartments that were themselves of the precise same proportions as the money too. Seeing so perfect a fit, it gave joy to the speller. *These* bills, however, were adorned with very different faces from those that Jasper held.

"Two hundred dollars."

"Yes, sir." He took it, backing away from the counter but then having to come back in order to put his name to a little chit of paper that described the date, the interest, the amount, and described Ben too.

Sixteen

Was he the man for it? To take these acres in hand and get a living from them? For there was no doubt but that he would be judged someday according to how he fared.

He used to work all day, all evening too, until the moon, slipping in and out of the clouds, made all further effort unavailing. Never had he been any good at sleeping, and now he began to give up the habit of it altogether. To be sure, he might *lie* for a certain number of hours, moving from the barn to the house and then back again, taking his blanket with him. Sleep, however, would not come. He had 180 specific worries in his head. And then too, the moon very often might emerge in sudden clarity, inspiring him to rise and dress and run out into the field, but only then to turn and come back again when the thing slipped behind the hills.

His wife was good at sleeping. He used to come in from time to time to check on her. In sleep, she had no bad taint about the mouth or eyes, no guile in any of her features. He had no criticism therefore, none, and yet . . . Sometimes he could not help but think that if only it had been in his fate to grow up and marry Belinda, could not help but believe that *she* would have come awake for him—such would have been her nature—and would be smiling back just now.

He went and looked in on Jasper, whose narrow cot was empty. Outside, the moon was in evil phase, displaying spots of mold in what might once have been a productive field. Suddenly, Ben screamed and lurched back in great horror, until he remembered that these were *scarecrows* on the horizon, (he had put them there himself), and not at all the two gaunt spirits that he had at first supposed. The night *was* nevertheless crowded; he could make out a delegation of crows passing overhead in an unsteady mile-long column in which each individual bird had been assigned to scan a certain square acreage of the earth. Ben hid. He did so love the methods of nighttime in this the darkest of all corners of the then-current Calaurian realm. Now again he spotted that location in the mountains where, night after night, someone had been signaling by means of a fire that blazed up brightly, only then to die away each time to nothing.

He went on, moving on tiptoes. He did not like to come too abruptly to the edge of the ravine lest he topple off in the darkness and then go tumbling the immense distance to the bottoms where, he knew well, there were Negroes dwelling on lands that were now technically his own. Here in this place on any given evening, he could hear, (but not see), all manner of things—doors slamming, the sound of moaning, a hog munching on walnuts. He had to grin at the effrontery of these people, an invisible community that thrived—he did not understand how—on the least possible exertion. Suddenly, that moment, and it was the third time that evening, he leapt back in great surprise. He had not seen that Jasper was just ten feet away, dressed only in his underwear. Lately, the man had been spending more and more of his time striving to read the future in the configuration of the cow manure when illuminated by the moon.

"The niggers is restless tonight."

"Shoot, I didn't even know you was standing there!"

"We could burn 'em out, I reckon—that's what your daddy would of done. 'Course, they'll just come right back."

Ben nodded. He had no wish to put fire to a forest that now was legally his own. "Shore wish I could sleep."

"Your daddy couldn't sleep. He and me, we used to . . ."

Ben waited for the story; instead, the man now changed his mind, preferring to keep silent. In front, a sheet of smoke was emerging gradually out of the valley, a ghostly page on which however nothing had been written. It snagged on one of the branches, stopping the view. From below came also the eternal smell of slop and bacon, of kindling, coffee, and charred pine. Ben was thinking he had come forth into history at the wrong time, and nothing before him but a long expanse of trials and tasks and infinite requirements that must eventually prove to have been quite futile, once he could look back upon them from the vantage of Jasper's age. Ben drew nearer, studying the man's satin-lined ear that looked as if it had been snipped off a calf and pasted to his odd-shaped head. At night, both ears hung down limply. One arm the man had, one only, the other having been blown quite away at Missionary Ridge.

"Just hope the weather holds," Ben said.

"Weather?"

"For the crops."

"Why, you don't know *anything* about weather! Why,

we used to—O, you Calaurians! Why, we used to . . . What the plague! Why, you don't have any idear of what I'm talking about. D'you hear? Burn 'em out! 'Course now, we didn't have no 'telephones.' Never needed 'em! Now your daddy's daddy, now *his* daddy, now *that* was a daddy! You, you wouldn't have lasted ten days! Not in *them* days. I thank my stars. No, no, *he* would of gone right into Hermione and snatched up any old gal he wanted!"

"She left the state."

"'State'? 'State'? There ain't any 'states,' boy! It's all in your mind. You just git yourself a yoke of oxen and *go*. And if they want to call it 'Arkansas' . . . well that don't make no never mind."

Ben said nothing. He knew how it was with this generation of men, and how they would always be hankering back for the Volcano Age.

"I expect that's right," said Ben finally. "But now I'm married to Betty."

"I know that! I knew it soon as I seen you riding up in that loaned buggy."

"And now I got to do what I can do."

"'What he can do.'" (He cursed softly under his breath.)

"I shore could use your help too."

"Well now! *There's* a true word."

"Shoot, I'll *give* you nineteen acres. Between you and me. And Betty doesn't even have to know about it."

The man looked at him, stepping closer. His eyes had a glittering quality made yet more aglitter by the signals coming from the hills. He was not drunk, not tonight.

"My wife," he said, "she used to own all of it."

"Yep. Queer, ain't it? And now *I* got it."

"You don't got it! Your wife's got it."

"But I got her."

The man cursed softly. Finally: "Nineteen, you say?"

"Shore! All that parcel that lies over against Mitchell's

place."

It seemed to satisfy him; he turned, spoke something that could not be heard, and then began to trudge back homeward. Ben knew him very well by now, and knew too that he would be spending the next minutes in his room alone while reporting back in a soft voice to his extinct wife about all that had happened on that day.

Seventeen

He woke, harkened to the sun, and then dashed forward to relieve the cow of her great burden that had turned overnight into high-butter-content milk. Even at a distance, her blue udder looked like a glove bursting at the seams, or as if a very fat hand had been inserted therein. Ben's own hand, these days it assumed naturally the milking grip.

He harkened to the rooster too, a tiny fowl whose voice, however, was larger than the world. Of dawn itself, Ben crouched down, expecting it to leap up in sudden aplomb behind Wooley's shack. The crickets were hoarse, or else had abandoned the field altogether, and meanwhile the last firefly of the night had been drawn into the pail and was struggling manfully to keep his little lantern above the surface of the milk. These were strange matters—night, dawn, lanterns. He knew too that he had only to look up into the sky—he did so now—to see all the greater confederate generals galloping past in the form of clouds.

He was waiting, concentrating upon the place where he expected the sun to come and turn the night to day. Instead, the sky itself began to show a certain number of hairline fissures, jagged as lightning. He thought, at first, the dome might actually turn to fragments and fall down on top of him. No place to run, the field was not broad enough. He shrieked, the generals were gone, the fissures broader. And that, of course, was when the sun jumped up behind Wooley's place.

He had much to do. Quickly he delivered the milk, passing it in through the open window where his wife sat waiting at the churn. Next the hoe—he liked to do this before the heat of the day. And then too, it was his practice to stroll to the fartherest end of the field and work his way back home again, his back turned to Mitchell who, more often than not, was doing his own hoeing just across the row of painted rocks that marked the boundary. They never spoke. Nor did Ben approve the other's style of hoeing. And yet, after five minutes, he found that he and the man were racing against each other.

Ben loved hoeing the least of all the tasks. Milking or spelling, planting or bee-work, he preferred them all to *this*. Half an hour of it and he began to feel pain in his broken liver. After a full hour, he began to sing, singing hymns. Very grateful was he when, toward eight, Jasper came out to help him, bringing with him a jar of spring water.

"Shore 'preciate it," said Ben.

"Mitchell!"

"I know it."

"Why, he's done twice what you done!"

Ben had to admit it.

"Should of shot that son-of-a-bitch long time ago. He's smiling too!"

They began to hoe in tandem. For ten minutes, the sun getting hotter, Ben refused to glance up from his work. He was able to see, (though he knew it already), that the soil was indeed full of things, evil things, some of them, and some that were said to be an aid to farmers. Of worms, he massacred more than was good for his soul, though without wanting to harm even one. As to

why these animals had selected to live *in* the ground instead of on the bright clean surface . . . Ben snorted in a
sort of amazed surprise. Even Jasper with his one arm
was a better hoer than was he. Jasper, however, had a
perfect liver. Finally, tossing the sweat from his face, Ben
now did glance up, shocked to see that Mitchell's wife
had come chasing down from her house and was assist-
ing in the competition.

They labored on, migrating down the row. Behind
them lay a long trail of severed weeds shriveling in the
light, whereas in front they were fast approaching that
awful patch that Ben had set apart from any agricultural
usage, knowing it to be full of sword fragments, of bones
and other things hard upon the tools. Three crows flew
over, their manure falling far off the mark of Ben, while
yet coming rather closer to the one-armed man. It promised to be ferociously hot today, the sun "gritting its
teeth," as it were, and "screaming" at them, so to speak.
And yet, all this was as nothing when compared to the
sun's full might and power that had been saving up over
the winter months. "Whew!" said Ben, halting long
enough to wipe his face with the great red kerchief that
he carried always. Jasper however said nothing. To say
such things as that, to him it signified the general wom-
anlyness of the modern age.

The hour drew on toward nine o'clock. Once, Ben
caught sight of a Negro boy spying out of the gulch who,
however, ducked back down again as soon as Ben pointed to him. Behind were hills, (smoke coming off the
summits), and in the far distance traces of dust and
powder where Mitchell and his wife were hoeing up a
storm. He could see much, Ben could, and what he discovered on this day was how each colored county was set
off neither by hue alone, nor yet by the ancient walls,

(which in any case were low enough that one could step over them), but rather by the type and chemistry of the encompassing soil. Here, he saw loam, and *there*, there a sandy sort of tilth in which only watermelons could expect to thrive. Suddenly, he stopped with his work, took out his glasses, and then bent somewhat closer to that "T"-shaped property, faintly pink, where Belinda once had lived. He was thinking about it, snorting in his way when, that moment, he saw what looked to him like a certain activity where the barn had previously stood.

He ran. Despite his internal injury, he found that he had lost neither his capacity for speed nor his skill for navigating across the furrows. His hoe, always kept bright, sparkled with a warning that shot across the field and hit the broken window in the vacant house with a shaft of light. Easily he leapt the wall and then, entering the neighborhood where he used to live, sped around the bend. The windmill that once had marked the precise corner of the county, now it too, like his own father's tower, had fallen into segments and lay in two different jurisdictions. Ahead, Belinda's house. It was still habitable perhaps, the greater part of it still covered by a roof. Ben leapt to the porch, leapt off it, and then dashed around to the back.

It was largely what he had expected—a white family of some dozen persons, and with a wagon that was loaded down under all manner of belongings. He counted three young boys, hard ones with worried faces; already they had formed up in line and were passing their things into the house. Ben reeled. The man too was hard-looking as well, and had a coating of tobacco juice about his mouth through which the growth of whiskers had with difficulty penetrated to the outside light. He wore the glum look of one who had not, and could not, and never would, leave poverty behind. Seeing Ben, he grinned weakly and took off his hat. Ben was not able to speak calmly.

"I see what you're doing. Hell, I could see from way over there!"

The three boys came running up, two on one side and one on the other. He would have to take on all four of them, Ben now realized, if he wished to take on the father.

"Yes, sir," said the man, "these are *my* boys. We're moving in today, sure are."

"I don't think so."

They looked at each other in a way that was still partly friendly, but also partly not. Finally, slowly, the man took out a slip of paper and passed it over to the speller, who could read such things easily. It proved that the man had paid his rent.

"Lord, I don't care about that!" said Ben. "See that fellow over there?" (He pointed to Jasper, who was working still and who, apparently, did not yet realize that he was doing it alone.) "A man like that, *he'll* shoot you."

"Now just hold on there! I paid! I paid good. And I plan to take what I paid for too." He pointed to his wife, a despondent-looking woman whose face had no expression in it whatsoever. Already she had gone into the house and now was bringing out her kettles and pots and replacing them in the wagon.

"Why Lord, I tell you I don't care about that! This is *Blinda's* place—you hear me? Now I recommend . . ."

He stopped. One of the boys, the middle one, had taken a .22 rifle from the wagon and was holding it in just such a way that no fair-minded person could claim that he was actually threatening with it. Was it loaded? The boy now aimed up into the air, as if he were targeting the crows.

"That boy of yours—I'd bet he's real good with that .22."

"They're *all* good. Clyde here, I guess he's the best."

Ben nodded. All those boys were hard, all of them wor-ried-looking, all of them adults. Clyde, Ben estimated, was not much more than fourteen, and yet had eyes . . . Ben did not rightly know how to describe them.

"You're paying twenty dollars the month to live in a place like *this*!"

"Yes, sir! Twenty."

"Give you thirty if you'll just turn around and go back where you come from. No questions asked."

"Thirty?"

"Right."

They drew off, the four men, in order to talk about it. It gave Ben the time to go and peek into the wagon and its load of trash. The family possessed any number of quilts, also an extra harness and what looked to be a dozen jars of canned vegetables. Two daughters, blond girls, were sleeping in the quilts. Ben checked the mules, sorry ones with sores and very little use left in either one of them. The men came back.

"Forty, and we can shake hands on it."

"Forty!"

"Yep. We *like* this place. Shade trees, and all that."

Ben cursed. A fourth son, far the smallest of the lot, now stepped out of the woods where, apparently, he had been relieving himself in Blinda's orchard. It came then to Ben that no sum was too much in order to be shut of such people.

He conducted them back to the farm and then, with the four sons, the two daughters and the woman all fol-lowing along by order of size, he ushered them past Jas-per, who noticed none of it. It meant the last of his sav-ings. To get it, he must now go over onto Mitchell's land and proceed some hundred rods toward a decayed oak in which some ten thousand hornets were living side by side in a scarce-concealed dislike for one another. Ben, who had a vocation for hornets, quickly filled the hollow with the green smoke from his pipe and then, probing daintily—the girls had run away—came out with a flat tin can that held, not forty, but rather fifty American bills.

"You keep your money in a place like that?"

"I do."

"Hey! who's *that* fellow?"

"Mitchell. He won't shoot."

"And . . . ?"

"Mitchell's wife."

They stepped across the line. The man, who was spitting out his tobacco juice at every third step, was thinking deeply. Finally:

"My boys and me, we could hoe this whole field, hoe it good too! Get it done by dinner time."

"I hain't got any money! *You* got it."

"You still got ten dollars. I know, because I saw 'em."

Ben groaned. The field *was* broad, the sun hot. And then too, it did seem as if the weeds were springing up anew almost as fast as Jasper could cut them down. He handed over the ten dollars.

It was three in the afternoon, the sun trembling with spite, before Jasper paused finally in his work. And although Ben was far away, he could see the hoe drop and could hear the old man's scream when he perceived at last that he had been toiling all this time, not with Ben indeed, but with a silent nation of blond people on all sides.

Eighteen

It never rained, and that night Ben had a dream about the field. He dreamt that it had grown larger, longer, flatter, broader, and that although he might crawl about on it in any direction, although he might inspect it with his nose not two inches above the surface, yet he never found the least evidence whatsoever of corn nor of cotton, nor of any good thing breaking through the skin. Suddenly, he turned and went crawling at terrific speed into the western quarter. If any moisture yet remained in any of his dirt, surely it would be here; instead, that was when he woke. Now once again, just as on every other night of his life, the great moon was seeping into his face. Far better it were rain, instead of mere light alone. Now, getting on all fours, Ben crawled quietly across the loft and then, coming down to within two inches of his wife's face, inspected it as well.

He had given away his last fifty dollars, nor had Jasper's bills come back into fashion yet. Therefore at 2:30 he stood and dressed and went out to the barn in order to ascertain that he was not absolutely without resources for the struggles that must come. (The land itself he no longer listed as a *resource* exactly, but rather an extension of his own person and self—180 acres of it, some in waste.)

In the barn he stood for some time, smoking in the dark until at last the animals grew accustomed to him and picked up whispering among themselves again. He could have wished that he might own ten such cows as this one, his demure and brown-eyed lady whose pointed horns Benjamin had burnished with so much care—she was far his noblest resource of all. By comparison, Betty's few hens were as nothing, birds of silliness, none of them possessed with sense nor with much of anything save a few eggs in the making—he could by no means trust to *them* to get them through the dry season. Ben thrust his lantern in amongst them. Nothing surprised him anymore; they seemed to imagine that it was sudden day, and that the lantern had become the sun.

Ben had no tractor—the times had not yet come to that. (Mitchell, a lewd man, had built himself a bathroom that was *inside his very house*, yet not even Mitchell had a gas-powered tractor as yet.) Instead, Ben thrust the lantern into the face of his mule, upon whose strength and gratuitous willingness all things now rested. They nodded, one to the other, Ben saying:

"Howdy. Going to be another hot one, they say. Hey! how come you ain't asleep?"

Ben continued on, followed by the two dogs that had recently emerged from the forest in order to join their fates with that of the speller and his family. Of these two, he counted one of them as a resource, but the other not. "Now listen here," he said, "I don't want *you* in this barn." Of course, as always, it was the wrong one who obeyed. If only he could speak to these things, the hens too, in a language that would go straight to the intellectual centers of their stubborn heads! *Then* might they see that he was not an unreasonable man, and took no joy in forcing his resources to behave in his (and theirs too) best interests.

He went outside. The stars, they were *not* his, not even those that lay over and directly above the field. No rain in prospect anywhere. Far to the West, the vestigial volcanos had weathered down by now to a series of mere hills that only very occasionally in these latter days still spat up from time to time a few red sparks. Nor did the other direction promise rain. And indeed, he had perhaps already witnessed in his "dry goods days" all the rain that he was ever likely to see.

He had a shed, and in it a few additional resources hardly worth describing. A hoe he had, in fact two, also an "adze," so-called, (he had no slightest idea as how to spell that word), and in the corner a wood-and-leather apparatus that Jasper sometimes used in lieu of the arm that he had left behind in Tennessee. Mallet, harness, ax, certain lengths of wood, Ben had these too, although it was nothing that could serve as collateral against a loan. He had a peck of flour and *some*, (but not very much—perhaps a week's worth) of chicken feed. He had a can of lard.

Slowly he moved back toward the house. Jasper's room, of course, was in confusion and filth, and although the man himself might be counted as a resource, yet the filth itself held nothing of any worth. Moving with stealth, Ben now strode to the open window and lifted out the two brown bottles of liquor, emptying them in the yard. Like Ben, the old man never slept. Instead, a peculiar sort of paralysis came over him each night, forcing him to lie with open eyes. He was not pleased to see his liquor being treated in this fashion, but yet remained too feeble to do anything about it, save to groan and roll his eyes. There were other bottles as well; Ben, however, knew better than to search for them in this black night.

Finally, he went down to check on his wife. As it happened, she was crumpled in just such a position as to let him look behind her ear. Now, working quickly, he struck a match and brought it down to get a better look. She had worked hard that day, harder than the men. And then too, she had burst a vein in the larger of her two hands. (The other, the smaller, it already had a hundred wounds, the hens having decided that it was the hand alone, and not the woman behind it, that had been taking their eggs.) Ben came nearer. There was no fault in the face either, though it was plain enough, morose even, and somberer in sleep than in life. He saw in it the 180 acres, of which those nineteen behind the ear were waste. She opened her eyes.

"Rain? Is it raining?" She started to get up.

"No, no," he said, "not yet. But it *might* rain. Now you go on back to sleep."

She obeyed. Her words about rain, they inspired Ben

to go out again and check the weather. There *were* clouds, but they were too far away toward the North to be of any interest to the Calaurians. Studying it, the formation, his mind drifted back to a certain theory described in his Commissioner's *Report,* in which the author had warned of that time when the earth's last and final rain would have come and gone, ruining the life of farmers. Ben smoked. He had set out three scarecrows, (even though as yet they had nothing to protect), and now one of them—or was it a living man?—was hiking across the field with what looked like an item of luggage on his head. Further yet, Ben was able to make out the very tiny figure of still another person, this one trundling hurriedly across Mitchell's place. In truth, there had been a considerable movement these recent nights, brought on by dry weather. And as if the land were not already dehydrated enough, the moon this night was full, high, powerful—it made his liver hurt. This moon however was *not* among his resources, nor had he ever tried to claim it. It belonged, he knew, to Alabama.

He gave it another half-hour, walking twice around the house and then lying in wait, hoping for a chance to leap out upon the next traveler in great surprise. No such opportunity came his way. Instead, toward four, he went, fetched a bit a string, and then contrived to make a muzzle for the rooster, in order that his wife might be vouchsafed yet two more hours of a good moist sleep.

Nineteen

On the thirty-first day, he hitched the wagon and drove away quickly, leaving behind him the old man who could not be trusted in the town. It is true that some of the people in his own county had now taken to automobiles, using them in the open roads. Ben therefore stood in the wagon, keeping a sharp lookout for the spumes of dust that showed when a car was on its way.

It was beautiful, in these days following the final rain; a grainy red haze suffused the earth. And when he came up over a rising, it was a good deal like the turning of a page in a book with maps and paintings in it. He saw a silo bending slowly to earth, and behind that the many squares and pastures set out in such ideal tidiness that the cows themselves were careful in how they kept it mowed. (He did not allow himself to glance toward Blinda's house.) Suddenly, a lizard, (but not *his* lizard) ran across in front, too small a thing to perturb the mules.

He went on. No automobiles interrupted the last part of his journey. He began to see the city spires and steeples, with droves of gulls wheeling in and out of the mass of children's kites. Those birds, they came, he knew, from the Sea of Mexico, there where the water, although salty, *never* went dry. On the contrary! It arrived in wave after blue-green wave, higher than a man—Ben had read about it.

When he came into the town, he found the people whispering on the corners, and still others standing out in the street itself. The sky was empty, no sign of rain. Even so, the farmers could not help but glance up every few seconds, some of them pointing to quadrants in the sky where the occasional whiffs of volcano smoke did bear some resemblance to true clouds.

"It *will* rain," said one, "but not until 'The Mule' enters the constellation of 'The 'Coon.'" Hey! here comes B. R."

B. R., however, standing in dignity, continued around the square. It saddened him to see that the ages-old goldfish fountain had evaporated completely, the fish themselves having no doubt flown away to that self-same overhead sky where shortly they would be forming constellations of their own. He preferred to ignore the four strange Negroes who, in any case, seemed to be having trouble hiding their glee. Today, it was the eldest had the glasses; to him, Ben finally did wave, whereupon the man burst into an outright cackling that was neither right nor seemly.

He drove around twice more, Ben did, passing in review the scenes of his dry goods years. Hattie's two daughters now had daughters of their own; they had all come out together to watch in consternation the farmers concentrating on the sky. Ben saw too where the *Last Chance Choir* had gathered on the courthouse steps, there to sing for rain—no one put much trust in them any longer. Ben moved past slowly, choosing not to look at them, and then finally parking and tethering his mules to a parked car.

This time Seth received him without the usual delays. The man had grown shorter over the past months, or else his desk was higher; he sat now, his jowls and wattle resting on the blotter.

"Ruined!" he said, "Oh, yes!"

"Sir?"

"Ruined, absolutely ruined."

"Wal! Me too, I'm ruined too."

"You? Well certainly *you're* ruined. But you're used to it, Ben, and me, I'm not."

Ben nodded.

"Me now," the banker went on, "now that's a *real* ruin, and a big one. Now if it don't rain tomorrow . . . I'm talking money, Ben, *money*."

"I know it."

"Thousand dollars a day—that's what I'm losing. What are *you* losing?"

"Well, I . . ."

"Don't talk to me about *that*, not when I'm talking about *this*. Thousand dollars an hour! How long you been here, Ben?"

"Sir?"

"I asked how long you been sitting here in my office. It's not a complicated question, Ben, really isn't."

"Well . . ."

"About thirty-five dollars' worth, *that's* how long."

Ben whistled.

"Now you see that trash over there?" (He rose to the window. He was not really shorter, but rather had an ailment in his back, or collapsing nerves, as Ben conjectured.) "That fellow with the whiskers? *Every one of those sons-of-bitches owes me money!*"

Ben looked. He would not have said that the whole bunch of them were trash. Abner yes, but not *all*. Ben said:

"I came to borrow another hundred."

"Ben, I've been dealing with trash all my life, and now *I'm* going to be trash too. Is it hard, Ben? You can tell me."

"It's right bad. Sometimes."

"I thought you'd say that. Goddamn it! Well just how 'bad' is it?"

"Well . . ."

"Hard on the liver, is it?"

They laughed, Ben too.

"What do you people *eat*, Ben? I mean: Do you ever have a nice piece of meat, for example? Things like that."

"Shore! Chickens."

"Chicken."

"Greens."

"Jesus." (He handed over the hundred, or rather handed over a check on which Ben could see that some six dollars of the amount had been subtracted to cover certain fees.) "Now Ben," the banker went on, "I want you to remember who it was that helped you, helped you when you was in such big trouble. Seth did. 'He helped me,'—*that's* what I want you to say to yourself—'helped me before he became trash himself.'"

"Yes, sir. He shore did."

"And if I should ever need some chickens, or greens, or . . ."

"Yes, sir; I'll see you get 'em. I shore will."

"Watermelons . . ."

"Yes, sir! Big ones."

They shook. Ben saw now that the man was wearing somewhat fewer rings than in old times, only one in fact. It bore a blood-red stone with the etching on it of a cobra emerging out through the dead eye of a horned skull. Again they shook, the man brushing away a tear that had only a short distance to fall before hitting the desk.

"The *toil*, Ben; how is *that*?"

"Shoot. You'll get used to that."

One tear more crashed to the blotter. They shook again, Ben meanwhile holding the check well out of view of the banker's fogged lenses and two bloodshot eyes. Seeing them, the anguished eyes, Ben wanted to weep himself. They shook.

He went direct to the government building. Here too, even as among Negroes, the Crop Specialist seemed to be overjoyed by the drought, its longevity, and many interesting complications.

"I *told* you to keep away from indigo? Didn't I tell you?"

"Yes, sir. I didn't plant no indigo."

"No? Actually, you could have done worse. What did you plant?"

"Corn."

"Oh! Oh! Oh! Jehoshaphat! And so now you've had to go to Seth, am I right? Corn!"

"Yes, sir. Cotton is seven cents."

"Keep away from cotton, Ben. I'm warning you."

"Yes, sir; I did. I kept away from it."

"Cotton however does not, repeat does not, spoil.

Corn, on the other hand . . ."

"Spoils."

"It can indeed; yes, sir. I've seen it happen."

"I've seen it too."

"As have I."

They looked at each other. Then:

"I reckon my wife's going to have a baby."

"Oh Jove. I warned you about that too—bringing children into weather like this. And who's going to do your wife's work?"

"Jasper?"

"Jasper's insane."

"Reckon I could *hire* somebody."

"Not me. I got to collate all this, everything you see, those papers, every bit of it." Suddenly, he leapt up and began rearranging his already very neat pile of informational bulletins, each bearing the federal insignia. He had also any number of plant specimens, some now in full bloom—they cluttered the desk, sill, safe, and all that part of the floor that did not lie in shade. Finally, blushing, Ben made the remark that had brought him to this interview in the first place.

"Need to make a loan," he said.

"Impossible. *We* make the loans. You, *you* don't make it; what you do is ask for it. Anyway, it's impossible."

"So's I can hire somebody."

"Not possible."

"What with all them acres of mine . . ."

"Nineteen are waste."

"And the baby."

"We don't make loans on babies, never, never. Look Ben, this here's the *Federal* Government. F-E-D-E-R-A-L. You used to be a speller."

"And so's I can buy another mule."

"No mules! Keep away from 'em, Ben, I'm warning you."

"Finish that barn. It ain't finished yet."

"'Barn,' you say? Yes, a barn is important."

"Shoot, it don't have to be a *Federal* loan; shoot, I could borrow it from you."

The man stood, sat, and then suddenly lurched up and ran to the window. "It's *my* money you want, I see. And why not my wife, my barn, you ever think about that? No. My babies? Come here, Ben; you see that trash out there?" (He motioned to the farmers loitering on the corners—the crowd had grown larger and appeared to be composed of enraptured star-gazers, to judge by how they were all craning to search the skies.) "Those clod-hoppers out there?"

"Yes, sir."

"Every stinking one of 'em owes money to the government."

"You don't tell!"

"Alright, Hattie doesn't owe. But all them others, they owe plenty, Ben, *plenty*."

"Yes, sir. I don't want to bother the government."

"You want to bother *me*."

"Yes, sir."

The man groaned. Ben knew this much about him, that at one time he had been affianced to Xenia, before Xenia had married outside the county. Ben said:

"Xenia's been poorly."

"I don't like to hear that."

"The weather, don't you know. It's hard on her."

"She's delicate."

"She shore is."

"Jesus. Alright, Ben, how much do you need? Don't be shy."

"About fifty dollars. More or less."

The man stood, sat, groaned, but then did take out, not a checkbook, but rather a cardboard wallet so full with receipts and photographs and the like that he had to go through the stuff item by item to select out the actual bills.

"Forty, Ben—take it, take it. I got babies too!"

"Shore do 'preciate it."

"You should. Now if I don't get it back by Christmas . . ."

Ben had to laugh. He knew full well it would not wait till Christmas before it rained.

"It'll rain before then. Bound to."

"Ben?"

"Sir?"

"It's got to rain before *another week is out*; otherwise, we're all dead men."

Ben nodded. He had counted the money and had put it away, keeping it distinct from Seth's check. That check, although smaller in inches, yet it was far grander in what it portended about the time between now and December.

He came to where the roads crossed and then, brushing past the Negro at the oyster bar, went up to the grocer himself, shaking hands with him.

"Benjamin Reuben. Everybody else is real gloomy, but not you, oh no. Why, Ben?"

"I came to make a loan."

"That right? Hey Willie! B. R. wants to borrow some money from you."

Willie stopped, (the oyster was almost to his mouth), and put on an expression of high alarm. "No, sir, Mr. Ben, I ain't got *no* money, no, sir."

"If I could just get *twenty* dollars, that's all. Or shoot, I'd take *ten*, if I could get it."

"That right? Me too, I'd take ten. Why, if I had ten dollars, why then I could lend it to Willie. And then Willie could pay me for some of them goddamn oysters he can't pay for."

"No, sir!" said Willie. "I paid. I paid last Febrery."

"My wife, she's fixing to have a baby."

"That right? It's your own fault, Ben. I thought Harold warned you about that."

"Now if I had just ten dollars . . . Shoot, I'll get it right back to you."

"That right? Let me tell you, Ben, your old-time *Hittites*—they were unquestionably the wisest of all those ancient peoples."

Ben waited for the rest of the story. The man had come down to the bottom of his keg of oysters, and yet Willie, his salt shaker held high, was by no means ready to leave. That was when Ben saw a new curiosity set out on the counter—a glassy fragment of volcanic basalt that was not however much more remarkable than hundreds of others that lay out alongside the highway. Finally:

"Well, I suppose you can have ten, Ben. But I'm going to need it back before Thanksgiving."

Ben had to laugh. The bill, when he got it, turned out to have the portrait on it of a man whose reputation in the county was not as low as formerly, nor yet so high as Washington's and his wife. To load this into his wallet without allowing the grocer to see that there was a fair amount there already . . . He elected to keep the stuff in his hand. For years he had been sniffing the scent of oysters, oysters and salt, never yet actually having had any taste of it. It was the closest he had ever been to the living sea.

"Shoot," he said. (Willie moved over for him, taking the far stool.) "Let me have one of them things."

"One?"

"The big one."

"No, Ben. That one isn't dead yet."

That was when Ben saw how Willie had taken out a small collection of change, a few dimes and nickels that he lay on the counter in front of him while he sought about in his pocket for the tobacco. Ben pointed, not to the smaller stuff, but to the quarter, nicotine-stained as it was.

"Lend me 25¢, Willie, if you would."

Of the oyster itself, it did have the aroma of the sea in it, the sea, the breeze, ships and whales. Having tasted of it, it seemed to Ben that there was nothing left now in the whole post-ancient world that he had not already done.

Twenty

It rained in Hermione, rained in abandoned Helice, and rained also in the North. In Calauria, where Ben's wife was getting plump, it remained as dry as heretofore. All might still have been well but for the rollicking sun, cruelest of all the stars; these days, it poured down upon them not with just "darts" and "arrows," but with buck-shot and even rifle ammunition. Accordingly, on the twenty-sixth day, Ben fainted. A long time he lay in the furrows, dreaming that his kidney was hurting, till Jasper came and pulled him home.

All might still have been well but for the well itself—the level of the water stood appallingly reduced. Working with care, Ben lowered the lantern until he came to the end of the string and then, peering and squinting and shielding his eyes, finally made out what looked to him rather like a squalid little puddle with slime on it, instead of the accustomed fund of blue-green "ink," (as he called it), from which his family drew their water. The toad, the toad remained, but looked back at Ben accusingly.

On the twenty-eighth day, Ben opened the gate and then, harnessing together the two cows, the mules, Betty's ewe, the dog and cat, led them all down toward the pond that lay on the disputed border between Mitchell's and Oldenfield's places. The distance, however, was great, and soon enough the dog broke loose and went back home.

Ben allowed his animals to drink but did not himself take any of it. In this way, he conformed to one of the county's earliest prohibitions. No one respected them more. Instead, he smoked. The pond was pleasant enough, hedged round with magnolia and pine. His beasts were too grateful to him to stray very far, and for a moment Ben almost dropped off to sleep. Even here, the pathetic breams must still lie constantly on their sides— the lake was that shallow. Ben dozed, but only to come awake very abruptly when he suddenly discerned a little old man, wildly bearded, sitting across on the opposite shore. Ben looked again. The man, dressed all in white, had pushed himself up into the air and had his whole weight, (which was by no mean great), on the palm of one hand. It was the oddest thing Ben had ever seen. He called:

"Howdy! I expect you must be Mr. Oldenfield. Howdy." Then: "They didn't drink much. Well! the cow now, she *does* drink an awful lot."

The man said nothing. It worried Ben, to see the way he lowered himself to earth and then, wrapping one foot behind his head, pushed back up into the air, staying there.

"It rained, they say," (said Ben), "in Phlius County."

"It hath not rained in Phlius County."

"Wal!"

"It hath not rained."

"My corn, it got about that high, high as you. Sun burnt it up."

"Oh, *I* see—you accuse the sun. And is it not always so? Calaurians? Blame this, blame that, anything suffices?"

"Sir?"

"You talk of corn. And yet, even as ye sit there uncomprehendingly, even now the Edge has begun to crumble beneath the heat. No, no, stay, stay; it's not a *serious* development, not yet. Just a few millimeters, nothing more."

Ben sank back down.

"However . . ."

Two crows flew over. Previously black, both had now greyed badly from lack of drink. Further still, a small blue puff of volcano smoke had stalled, indeed had stopped, and would drift no more.

"You ain't Oldenfied. Are you?"

"Automobiles called 'cars,' 'tricity, trains, and telephones. Yesterday I saw a man riding on a machine."

"That would be Mitchell. 'Course now, he's got five hundred acres, near about."

"Universities, and things in Europe. You'll be pleased, I must suppose, when Calauria has 5,000 souls in it? Each riding on a machine? How then, with all that clamor and doings, how *then* will ye halt the Edge from unraveling altogether, ha? No! It was not for this that I came all this way, from 'world to world,' as we say, certainly not. Blundering down through the epochs." Then: "How's Jasper?"

"Lost his arm."

"So."

"In the war."

"War? See what I mean?"

Ben hummed. It had astonished him to find that yet a third man had been cooling his feet on the far side of the pond; now, taking up his chair and his straw hat, this person rose, turned, and strolled away in high annoyance. Ben waited until he had disappeared over the furrows.

"Sir?"

"Ah?"

"This dryness . . ."

"Call this dry, do you?' (He laughed, a hissing sound that made him vibrate somewhat in his unsteady stance. Ben could not have said what sort of robe he was wearing, all sky blue, and with the symbol on it of the cow's skull with empty sockets and snake.) "No! In your *true* dryness, you wouldn't have your little ponds, like *this* little pond, nor your little fishes on their sides."

"Like *these* fishes?"

"Just so. Your true dryness is a killer of cities—oh yes! I've seen it—and spreads like a contagion, leaping across interstices, and of worlds. See there?" (He pointed, pointing crookedly to a certain sector in the sky where there was nothing that Ben could perceive. It left the man teetering on but one support alone—his extraordinary left arm, thin but strong.) "See? That too was a flourishing place once. But I wouldn't go there now, not for all the hay and fodder in . . . How do you call this realm? Choctawia?"

"Alabama."

"Ah yes. And now I'll have my nap. I mean with your permission, of course."

"Shore." Ben left him. The ewe had wandered far, even to the horizon itself, which proved so much huger than the animal had expected. Ben must hurry lest, (temptation proving too much), she turn and go that way.

Twenty-one

Days did pass. Or rather, one whole month during which the development of his corn was that of days only. Unwilling to look at it in daylight, he used to wait until full dark before taking his lantern and crawling with it to this or to that locality of the field. He discovered that the stalks were higher where the soil was thinner, which is to say five inches tall as compared to two. One little plant indeed had come up with a luxuriant tassel, like a youth who had died while wearing a manly moustache. He saw no formation anywhere of actual cobs, nothing in which the kernels might otherwise have found a footing.

Toward midnight, sometimes he crawled to the fence and even beyond it. Here, out of sight of the man's home, he could inspect Mitchell's cotton in more detail.

"Why, there ain't even any bowls!" Ben said.

"There ain't no bowls over here neither," said Jasper, his lantern resting somewhat askew.

"Five hundred acres of nothing! This is liable to be the end of *him*."

They grinned.

"And now maybe he'll be willing to talk to us."

"Doubt it. Hell, he'd sell his wife before he'd turn loose of just one of them acres."

They crawled past each other, Ben going forward to inspect the sorghum and Jasper the rice. Concerning rice, Mitchell's attempt at it had been a perfect failure. But Ben's greatest joy came from not finding one single sorghum tree among the weeds.

"Nothing!" he called. And that was the moment, of course, when the baby arrived—a cry and a yelp, and then silence from the cabin. "Hee!" said Ben. "Can't do sorghum in Calauria County, no sir!" Suddenly, he ducked down low. The moon had this way about it—that some clouds (or was it smoke?) were simply too tenuous to hold back the light. Jasper, for example, was easily to be seen. And then too, there was signaling from the hills, all which added to the general illumination. The very last that Ben wanted now was for Mitchell to come forth and find them there, implicated in an acreage that belonged to someone else.

They gathered in the cabin. The old man now smoked very nearly as much as did the speller. They sat, both thinking deeply, both of them despondent. The old one had enough memories of his own, wherefore Ben opted not to afflict him with further bad news about the Edge. So many insects; they gave off a smell, leaping thus impatiently into the flame. Once only they heard a bitter cry—but not from Betty—(she never cried)—from the adjoining room. Finally, Ben did rise and fill his pipe again and then, to appease Jasper, began to read out loud from his agricultural *Yearbook*.

It never failed: The old man sat up straight, absorbing the information "head on," as it were, and with no intermediaries. Ben read slowly however, pausing from moment to moment to glance at the man's pained expression. So much knowledge, a wisdom so deep—it was a cruelty to point out in this way all the things and procedures that the old man had never known.

"Wal!" he said. "I never!"

Ben went on, page after page until suddenly, without warning, he broke into Lippincott's essay concerning the atmosphere. For Jasper, it was too much. Ben too, he was by no means so certain that he understood *all* of it. It was four o'clock in the morning. Both men smoked. The moon itself was dilapidated, its power largely gone and even its very shape more like that of an egg than of any normal moon at all. Finally, with the clock showing 4:22, Ben got up, closed off the curtain, and then went into the adjoining room.

He had to wait a good while for his vision to adjust. As to the woman, she appeared to be asleep. Ben came nearer, probing into the covers, finding the child finally, a small one, and then leaping back suddenly in great surprise. She had created a mess, the woman had—it was not like her—and Ben could not absolutely discern the baby from the goo.

Twenty-two

Came winter, winter in Alabama; they lived primarily on potatoes and greens. The Alabama greens gave four varieties—mustard, kale, cabbage, and that fourth sort whose name Ben was forever forgetting. Even the potatoes put forth two kinds. He used to take the sweet ones and eat them whole, never discarding the skins. And refused to go abroad without two or three warm ones in his underwear.

One by one, they consumed the chickens. And yet, the more they followed this approach, fewer the eggs. No one came forward wanting to lend further money, no one. As a result, Ben's whole family began to shun the town. He had very small chance now of buying off any significant part of Mitchell's place. On the contrary! he once caught Mitchell leaning over the fence and, with his wife and baby, (a baby somewhat larger than Ben's), caught all three of them gazing with yellow eyes upon Ben's own poor barren plot, full still with stunted corn. As for the scarecrows, having nothing to do, they had decamped long ago, filing away one by one, their shirt sleeves rattling in the wind. He never saw them again.

In winter, the rains having come back, he began to spend much of his time in the barn. It was here, next to the cow's apartment, that he had begun to fabricate beehives out of the odds and ends left over from the burnt house. Thus, the hives themselves varied widely in size, in form, and in the amount of care he gave to each several one. His theory was that the nobler the hive, the better-built it was, the more the little insects would strive to measure up to it, even sometimes to filling them to overflowing with the local orange-colored honey that possessed such amazing heaviness. That was why Ben strove as hard as he did to build as skillfully as he could. Jasper took no part in it. *His* way was to stomp on bees, rather than to cultivate them. And then too, with his single arm and his non-coordinated eyes, Ben tried to keep him away from carpentry. So he sat, watching suspiciously while the speller nailed and painted and, as often as not, disassembled the things in order to put them back together again in better fashion.

He was there still when November came in, and the most enormous rains in memory began to fall. On such dire nights, he thought that he could hear his own land breaking off in the downpour and crumbling over the Edge. He still could see the house from the barn however, even if the rain was too heavy to let them try and dash across the distance.

Two days went by. Several times his wife tried to signal to him, placing the lantern in the window. Finally on the third day, a thin trail of smoke—it was December now—could be seen coming from the chimney. Her supplies of food and firewood were adequate, whileas for the men, they had the chickens with them. Jasper knew how to cook eggs over smoldering straw, a diet that sorted well with the sweet potatoes that Ben had also hoarded away at places both inside and outside the barn.

They would not starve, not this year, not even if it rained continuously and if Ben and his wife had to go the whole time communicating by lanterns only. One great dread did weigh upon him—that the river, which was far away and had never been known to achieve flood stage, that it might nevertheless come broaching up silently when he least expected it, and might float away his barn, wife, cow, himself and all.

"The river . . ."

"There ain't no 'river'! Anyway, it's all in your mind."

"Mitchell's house . . ."

"Gone!"

They grinned. He had built on low ground, Mitchell had, and by the time his house came finally to rest, he would have a long walk back to his acres, assuming those acres had not also broken off and gone down into the Mexican Sea.

"Well!" said Ben. "I just don't see how I can get to town, not in all this rain, sure don't, don't rightly see how I can get to town and pay Seth what I owe him."

"Be dry tomorrow."

"Tomorrow!"

"And Seth, he'll be here on Wednesday."

Ben hummed.

"You betcha. He'll want about forty acres. Thirty, if he's feeling real kindly. The surveyor, he'll be here too."

Ben, who had been heating an egg, now opened the thing and consumed it, humming still. Jasper went on:

"*My* land. Used to be mine. 'Course now, that was before my daughter, or grand-daughter, went and got herself ruint by a goddamn speller! Ruint! And there wern't no honor in it neither. And me at my age."

"Rhys, I owe him too."

"Rhys."

"A little bit."

"I reckon next thing you're going to tell me you owe *Willie Smoot* too."

"And Harold."

"Harold. He's been wanting this land for a long, long time. How 'bout Hattie, how much *she* getting? I tell you, we ain't going to have enough left so's we can keep both feet on it!" (He lifted one foot and began hopping about on it, showing Ben how it would be. Any third party, watching them, would have thought a celebration was going on. Ben went back to his hives.)

With the floods finished and Christmas coming in, Ben rose early, dressed, saddled the mule, and then, without mentioning anything to anyone, drove out past the gate and down past the place where Mitchell used to live. (He hardly dared to turn and look at the next farm-stead, the best of all places, where once he had passed his best of all days.) The valley itself had been hollowed out by floods, and he was able to marvel at barns resting on their gables, and further, a warehouse broken open and strewing a mile-long deposit of cotton that extended to the sea. The roosters were confused; one of them came even to the road and stood there, staring at Ben with an indomitable pride together with accusations. To his shame, Ben had allowed himself to hope that the bank too might have washed away, carrying the banker with it. He did see bits of clothing hanging in the branches, also an automobile, costly beyond belief, and yet unable to float.

He came gingerly into town and then drove two times around the square. Very few people had ventured to come outside, and even those cast very faint shadows. He would have said it was a city with not more than fifty souls in it, instead of the four hundred that had tenanted there in times before the dryness and the flood.

Ben parked, tying his mule to a mule that someone else had parked. The bank was nearly empty, aside from a farmer who was slowly and sadly emptying out his overall pockets and placing the objects one by one on the counter, where the clerk could make a record of it. Now came Seth, his hand already primed for a handshake, un-til he saw that Ben's hand was somewhat unclean.

"Benjamin Reuben! All one hundred and eighty of you. Oh, yes. And did you bring the papers?"

"Thought I might like to borrow a hundred and fifty dollars, if it's alright."

The man looked at him in astonishment.

"Dollars?"

"Yes, sir. My wife, she's going to have a baby, and so I shore could use . . ."

"Baby? Well how long is that baby going to be shilly-shallowing around—that's what I want to know. Why Lord, he's been in there a year!"

"No, sir; this is a *new* baby."

"New, oh."

"And so I shore could use . . ."

"Collateral, Ben, what are you going to put up for collateral?"

Ben thought. The two babies sprang to mind, followed by the mule.

"What did I use last time?"

"Your name, Ben, your good name. And now that's all gone. No, I thought you came in here to *pay* me, not ask for more. My goodness." He sat back—he seemed taller than just of four months ago—and took up his cigarette, a long one packed full with little grains of black explosive tobacco. "Ah yes," he said, "this weather has been awfully good to me, Ben. I suppose that's the way it should be."

"Yes, sir."

"*Foreclosing*, boy! Here, there. Hell, we even been foreclosing over in *Hermione*. You remember that place, don't you Ben?"

"If I just had a hundred dollars . . ."

"No, sir. According to my calculations, you already owe quite a pretty little pile already."

"Yes, sir. I figured if I signed over them nineteen acres . . ."

"Nineteen? You mean forty, don't you?"

"Yes, sir. Forty."

The man laughed merrily. "Now I tell you what—you hand over that forty, and that will still leave you with . . ." (he used his pencil). "Well hell, according to my calculations that will still leave you with one hundred and another forty American acres. That ain't bad, Ben! No, I'd say you're a lucky, lucky man, everything considered."

Ben grinned.

"A *very* lucky man. Now let me ask you this, Ben: Are you also a *gambling* man?"

"I used to be."

"Oh?"

"But I couldn't never figure out where the pea was."

"Are you *still* a gambling man?"

Ben could feel his heart begin to thump. Danger he sensed, a feeling akin to that as when he had first heard about the unraveling about the Edge.

"I *might* gamble. I *could*."

"Well alright then! Look here, I'll give you that hundred—hell, let's make it *two* hundred—now that's fair ain't it?—and if you can't pay me, pay by next Christmas, well then I'll have to have all them acres. All. How does that sound?"

"Nineteen is waste."

"I know that. You can keep those, Ben. See? We call it *integrity*, people in my circle do. If you lose, my integrity will let you keep nineteen. Now how's *that*?"

Ben had to grin. He knew so little about the other man's circle. Finally, they did shake on it, although Ben found the banker's hand to be perhaps the strangest he had ever touched. It reminded him of a certain oleaginous turnip that he had dug one time from his garden, and had to throw away.

Ben went off straightway, striding past the secretary while trying not to disclose the arrogance he actually felt, owing to the cash in his pocket. The mule, however, was gone; Ben found him on the other side of the square where, apparently, he had been trying to identify the route that would carry him home again. By hap, the wagon had come to a halt just in front of the government office.

Ben went up, knocked and entered. The flood had come up even to the second story level, and had floated away a good many of the man's potted specimens. The agent himself sat slumped in his chair, his face a study in absolute pessimism taken to extremes.

"I *warned* you," he said. "Rains and floods."

"No, sir! You never did."

"If God loved the farmers, you see, He would of made it damp in June and dry in November. But oh no; God *hates* unfortunate people. Hates you too. Don't you see that, Ben?"

Ben had to grin. He had not meant to do it; nevertheless, he now took out the two hundred and spread them across the desk where the man could not fail to see them. The response was not what he expected. The agent leapt up, a wild expression in his eyes.

"Oh, no, no, no, say it isn't so, Ben, no, no. Gambling with that son-of-a-bitch? Oh, no, no, no; I guess He hates you even more than I thought. Let me ask you this, Ben: How will you know if you've won your gamble?"

"Why, if I can pay him back, why then I *win*."

"And what do you win?"

Ben thought. All his life he had been above the average in spelling, in reading, and the associated skills. Not so in the area of mathematics and/or games of chance. Indeed, he still had a lingering bitterness for that day when he had thrown away so many of Memnon's dimes.

"Ben, Ben, Ben."

"Maybe I could borrow it from *you*."

"Ben, Ben."

"Or from Claude."

"Claude's ruined. Got foreclosed. Would you want to guess who foreclosed on him, Ben?"

Ben sank back down. Already his mind had retreated to his own residual acres, waste ones, and whether or not he could derive a living from just nineteen.

"Ben, Ben, Ben. Who told you to be a farmer? There's just no future in it, not with cotton at six cents."

"Got my bees."

"Ben, Ben."

"Got my hens."

"How many?"

Indeed, they had eaten the last of them.

"You need a *position*, Ben. Take me now, *I've* got a position. See?" (He stood.) "And I'm not near as good a speller as you."

Ben nodded, his imagination suddenly running rampant over his spelling days, before the knowledge of drought and floods had come into the world.

"Position."

"Exactly. I think Xenia would have wanted it for you."

Ben's imagination turned to Xenia, dead these seven weeks. He had not visited at her funeral, no one having thought to invite him.

"Yep, reckon she's starting to rot by now."

"Shut up, Ben. God! I knew her when . . . Hair down to her waist. Alright, you might as well know it—I was sweet on that aunt. Didn't you ever wonder why I'm the way I am? Jumping up and down all the time?"

Outside, the courthouse clock, stopped with debris, was trying vainly to strike the hour. They smoked in silence, Ben and the man. Not so long ago, it was the man who used a pipe and Ben raw tobacco; now it the other way around.

"Position."

"Yes, sir."

"*Government* position. They're the best."

Ben nodded.

"But you'll have to take a test. No, that's the way we do things now."

"Yes, sir. I was just thinking: What kind of test is it?"

"Well! They tell me it's mostly about *spelling*."

They looked at each other meaningfully.

Ben went straight hence, riding in dignity about the three sides of the square. It was obvious that the four weird Negroes were without their spectacles—there they sat, back to back, squinting off into the four directions. It was when Ben came to the end of the block that he saw a small child blundering about blindly, the very glasses on his head.

Now that he had two hundred dollars in his pocket, he stopped to give some of it to Claude. And then too, although Ben had always thought of him as a rich man, he *was* curious to see how he looked in his foreclosed state.

"Howdy!" he said. Suddenly he reached for the money, drawing it out with a bored indifference.

"Keep it, Ben; put it back. I'd just have to hand it over to our . . . 'leading citizen.'"

"You don't tell!"

"It's true, Ben. My wife left me too. See how it is? Everything goddamn thing I got, Seth's got it now."

"Well tarnation, he's already got one wife!"

"Stock, receivables, it's all his, all." Suddenly, his voice grew especially loud: "Ain't that right, Willie?"

Ben looked to Willie, finding that he was gulping the oysters at great speed. The oysters too, apparently they had been foreclosed as well.

"It's God," said Ben. "I reckon He just don't care about unfortunate people."

"That's blasphemy, Ben; I'm surprised at you."

"What you need is a *position*. There ain't no doubt about it."

"I got a position! It's just not any good. And if anybody in this world needs a position, it's you Ben, it's you."

"My wife's going to have a baby."

"Well. I don't blame *her*, no, I blame *you*. You, Ben, you; *you* did it. It's always you."

Ben looked off.

"Now if people like you would just stop that whole business, messing about and whatnot, why then there wouldn't be any problems, not here, not anywhere."

"Left you, you say?"

They looked at each other. Heretofore they had gotten along well with each other; now instead, the man drew himself up and then, putting on the "foreclosed expression" that Ben had expected in the first place, went off to help Willie get the shells open.

Twenty-three

He dreamt that he was already in the test, that it was exceedingly difficult, that he was *not* doing well, and that soon enough, he who once had wanted to distinguish himself in front of the county, instead his failure would be known in every home and farm. Twice he groaned, very loudly, perturbing both the babies and his wife as well. In the dark, no one could see that he was grinning, ashamed of his own nerves and his folly. Finally, toward two, he rose and took the blanket, and went out to the barn.

Again, he dreamt that he was in the test. The test did have ciphering in it, but not nearly so much as of spellings. All might therefore have been very well, if only he had been given a pencil with a point on it. And even then, even after he had gnawed it down—no graphite!

Ben groaned. In his fever, he had come to think that some of the answers might be written in the sky; accordingly, he ran back toward the house and began furrowing about in the bureau until he came up with the pair of antique glasses, very powerful ones, that his grandfather had used. Was this still a dream? In any case, the moon was gone. That was when his wife sat up in bed.

"Nobody," she said, "knows as much as you about spelling and writing and such."

"Numbers. There's liable to be lots of numbers on that test."

"Oh." She rose, put on her robe, and went to make coffee. Only now did Ben see that she was again pregnant. (He speculated that this time, to judge from her, she had *two* babies forming at the same time, one of them slightly senior to the other.)

"And not just ciphering neither; they're going to want some *mathematics* too."

"Wear them extra socks," she said. "And then if it gets real cold, why you'll be warm."

"Trig'nometry."

"And take that knife of yours too. And then if you burst one of them pencils, why you can get it all sharp again."

"I always take it."

"I'll boil some eggs. 'Case you get hungry."

"*We* never had eggs," said Jasper. "'Course now, we never needed no route postmen neither!"

Ben looked at him. The man had brought his false arm to the table and was sitting on it. It was useless to say anything about his bad habits, or that he allowed the cat to eat out of the same dish with him.

"Seth gave me some more money."

"'Gave'? Why you damn fool. He never 'gave' you no money! He didn't *give* it, no sir! And now he's going to want the whole place!"

"Not if I can make the grade on that examination."

"There ain't no 'examination'! That's *government* talk, boy."

"My sister has a place," said Betty. "I know she'd take us in."

"I ain't staying with no sisters! And I ain't doing any more hoeing neither. I quit."

"Claude got foreclosed."

"And wear your hat too—liable to be raining, the ways things have been."

"I didn't tell you—it's twenty-five dollars the month, that's what it is, being a postman. *Every* month."

"I should of shot that son-of-a-bitch dead!" said Jasper, who now once again was thinking of some old episode.

"Each and every month, and all of it backed up by government writ."

"I swear! He's got his tongue in that honey *again!*"

"I'm sick," said Ben.

Suddenly the baby, the one that was "in the world already," began bawling in the next room; it excited the rooster who began to crow, and this in turn brought up the sun.

"But I don't know if it's where he hit me, or if I'm just plain sick."

"Them honey flies of yours, they been biting on you too much. You ain't sick."

"Well. If you're going to the doctor, I better go too," said Betty. "He told me to."

"Told you?"

"Why yes. 'You come see me,' he said, 'when you get to be sixteen.'"

"Well you're a whole bunch older than that! Tarnation, you was older than that when the house burnt down!"

"If he'd of hit *me* like that, I'd of killed him for sure. Still ain't too late."

"I'm worried," said Ben, "about those babies. The big one is setting on top the little one—that's what I think. What kind of man is he going to be, after all that?"

"My lands. That's the *second* time that sun has

jumped up like that. Seems to me"—she pointed—"it ought to be over yonder."

"It's all this wet. Look, it's raining right now."

The true dawn did finally come, whereon the three of them, huddling under the blanket, got aboard the buggy and then, after splashing down the lane, turned and drove back and locked the three dogs inside the barn. These were emotional dogs, and they dreaded to see the woman who fed them, to see her leave.

It was a rainy day in every way; already, the river was beginning to rise. Ben loved to see how it cooked up a mist that rolled and tumbled and that seemed to take such delight in having been called into being. It was a desolated world, nor did the crows still gloat in quite the same old way. Himself, Jasper had seen something floating in the river, a cow or wagon or something of like size, and was so intent upon it that he ignored the rain. Not so Ben and his wife; they were forever adjusting the blanket, striving to keep themselves dry, as also the lunch in its uncovered basket.

It was as if the doctor had been waiting for them. He sat, distinguished-looking, waiting on the screened-in back porch where he had his telephone, his microscope, his tools, medicines, and mounted photographs of the well-known people he had cured. Among others, Ben saw the current congressman, a heavy man, Seth's friend, pictured here with a thermometer in his mouth.

"Benjamin Reuben. Brought your family, I see. Yes, and I'm especially mad at you, Betty."

"I *wanted* to come. It's the hens."

"Hens."

"We had to eat them."

"That how you got so fat?"

"That ain't fat!" said Jasper. "Them's *babies* in there."

"Ah! So *that's* where you keep them." He had a stethoscope and was running it over her belly. "I'm trying to see if I can find a heartbeat, Betty."

She paled. Never had she imagined that a person could *see* with an instrument of that kind.

"You're low, too low!" said Jasper.

"It worries me, doctor," Ben said, "about the new one. Getting squished in there all day long."

"I see! Well maybe we ought to change 'em around, put the tiny one on top for a change."

Ben nodded enthusiastically. Betty had lost interest in the stethoscope and was reaching out, trying to stroke the drapes, which did have a deep velvet nap on them.

"Yes, sir," said Ben, "I'm thinking I might want to take up a *position*, you understand. Government position."

"Just now I'm looking at your wife, Ben. We'll do you next."

"Didn't have any steth'scopes in *my* day. Just didn't need 'em, I reckon."

"Betty, when I die, I'm going to see you get that curtain." Then: "Open your mouth." Then "When was the last time you saw a dentist?"

"Now I'm not saying now that I'm going to make the grade," said Ben, "leastways not the *first* time. Shoot, I can take that test hundreds of times."

"You got yourself a good strong wife here, Ben, if you take care of her. How old are we now, Betty?"

She thought. She still had her hand on the curtain.

"Eighty! Or near 'bout it."

"No, no; how old is *Betty*? I already know about you."

"Hit me right . . . here!" said Ben, pointing to that spot. "And it's been hurting ever since."

"Yes, and you're still smoking that cow manure too. I told you about that, Ben." He accepted the sandwich that Betty passed him, but peeped inside it before tasting the thing. He seemed pleased. "It's true that I like cucum ber," he said. "You should too. Why is Jasper out there in the yard?"

They looked. The old man had seen something, or perhaps was just generally curious; now he lumped past the window, uttering to himself.

"Pays twenty-five dollars the month," said Ben. "And that's every month, don't you see."

"Now Ben, I'm going to give you something, and I want you to take it every single day. Calomel. Lots and lots of lovely pink calomel. It tastes like dew. And it's good for your pancreases too."

"No, sir, it's my liver. That's where he hit me."

"No, Ben, it's your pancreases. They need draining."

Ben took the medicine, a tall narrow bottle of it that the man dug out from the neatly-stacked socks and shirts that he kept in his bottom drawer. Ben saw too some half-dozen fishing lures, mint-new seemingly, all of them still packaged in little oblong boxes with cellophane. One was a joke no doubt, because it was in the shape of a little blue mermaid with actual breasts. Ben feared that his wife might see it.

"You too Ben, you ought to see a dentist too. Think of it like this: 'How many teeth do I have left?' and 'How long will they last?'"

Ben looked off. The calomel *was* pinkish, thicker too than honey; he had expected it to taste far, far better than in fact it had. That was when the doctor yelled at him.

"Great God A'mighty! Ben? I never meant you had to drink it all *in one day!*"

"Well shoot, I can make it last for weeks, the way it tastes. And I plan to pay you too, just as soon as Seth and me get all settled up."

"You and Seth; Jesus Christ. Now Ben, I want you to . . ."

The telephone rang.

"I reckon that's your telephone," said Ben. "Or 'radio.'"

"Good, Ben, that's good; I can see you know all about these kind of things. Now I want you to come back real soon, you hear? When Betty gets to be thirty, or nearly."

Twenty-four

It came time for Ben to take his civil service test. In his mind, he half-expected to find the mayor waiting for him on the courthouse steps; instead, the delegation consisted of a single man, a meager sort of person with thinning hair. Ben parked, got down, and was tying the mule to the lamp post when the examiner ran forward to him.

"Mr. Yaeger? You're late, quite late; I'm surprised."

"Howdy."

"I don't know about this—being late. Well, come along, come on. Tell me, Mr. Yaeger, the people on your route, do you plan to make them wait too? The taxpayers? They won't."

They all entered the courthouse together and began to push down past a crowd of litigants who had come to town—Ben knew all about it—over some old boundary dispute. No mayor. By habit, Ben headed off toward the room where he used to teach spelling, until the man pulled him back.

"Gracious! Ah well, you know what they say."

"Yes, sir."

"'Those who start out badly.' Well! Sometimes they end up doing real well after all. Let's hope so. Now your wife, she can't go with you."

Here, Ben had to laugh. "Why I can't go taking no test with all them children crawling all over me!"

"Nevertheless . . ."

"And *she's* got the basket."

The proper room turned out to be small, low-ceilinged, the same cell, as Ben began to suspect, in which the modern hangings were carried out. Very few chairs. Ben was saddened to see that another man had gotten there before him and was hunched over the table with poised pencil, as if waiting for the starting gun. However, Ben knew in his soul that he could have thrashed this person easily, his own diseased spleen notwithstanding. They glared at each other, till the man weakened and looked away.

"And now if we can all be seated . . ."

"I brung my knife," said Ben, showing it and casting a look over at the other test-taker. "But I just plan to use it on the pencils, that's all."

Already his wife had spread the cloth and already had taken out the chicken wings and biscuits. The two boys had gone up immediately to the window, but only the taller one was actually able to peer over the sill. Ben smoked. He was evaluating the back of his competitor's head, which might well be full of brains indeed, to judge by it. And all this time the thinning man, his smudged glasses moistened by a kind of fussy nervousness, all this time he was trying to get his papers into a more coherent order. Ben spoke, addressing himself to his own children:

"Now I don't want you boys poking at this gentleman. Bothering him. Not when he's trying to take an important test."

The man flushed, peeping back bashfully at the boys, at the woman, and at the food spread out over the next table. The proctor had given each of them a set of papers which, however, they must not glance at as yet, not until the gun. Ben used the time, first, to smite his eldest-born upon the rump, (the boy was behaving badly), and then secondly, to take up one of the chicken wings. Betty was sewing happily, and at the same time humming her favorite hymn. Her mind, however, was ranging far afield, as Ben could see by looking at her.

The "gun," when it went . . . In fact, it took the form of the proctor simply uttering the command. So agitated was the other man that he immediately began heaving and swooning, and seemed near to breaking down altogether. It gave Ben the advantage. These questions about the English alphabet, the succession of letters, their hierarchy, formation, their transmogrification when in the upper case—all this he knew to perfection. He felt indeed that he had set sail in sweet weather upon that very "sea" that he had never personally viewed, that he was sailing well and soon would be slipping into berth at deadfall, calm harbors, harbors of the mind. He smoked. Soon enough, he knew, storms must come, thrusting him out onto the high ocean once more, mathematical oceans of the mind. But it was while he was still in the alphabet that Betty turned to check his face, finding it serene. It made her serene too, whereon she began to sing, instead of merely humming.

How the hours did go on, both of them, both going. And when it came time for the mathematical parts, he was already hardened for it. He who had stood up to Cletus and the others, it was no error on his part to have believed that he could also crush multiplying problems simply by way of an advanced tallying of his arithmetical skills. His complacency put on new growth. The bashful man, having refused drink, wings, all of it, was plainly suffering now. It came then to Ben that he might be able to help the fellow later on, by allowing him to deliver at least a part of the route.

He toiled, late into the day; the other man had gone away. He found, Ben did, that out of all that long list of alphabetical characters, he never confused any of them, saving only "U" with "V," which had given pause even to the ancient Romans. Finally he stood, brushed the crumbs out of his lap, and called for the proctor, who came running.

"Well, reckon I'll take my leave now."

"Finished, are we? What happened to Mr. Schönst?"

"Reckon he quit." (Ben could not help but smile.)

"Quit! You didn't . . . ?"

"No, sir! I never laid a hand on him, no sir."

"Never," said Betty.

"They tell me I get a uniform too."

"What? But we haven't scored you yet."

"Twenty-five green dollars the month. Whew!"

He was extremely happy; moreover, down below, his eldest had gotten into a squabble with one of the town boys, and it was clear enough who was getting the best of it there too. Again he stuck out his hand for shaking, again the thinning man simply touched it, his own hand leaping back before Ben could get a grasp on it.

"That boy of yours is causing quite a little commotion down there, Mr. Yaeger. I knew you'd want to know."

Ben blushed with modesty. "I got another one coming along too," he said, pointing to his wife's belly.

"Really? Now Mr. Yeager, you'll be . . ."

"Maybe two."

"Good, good. Now Mr. Yaeger, you'll be getting your results . . ."

"Blue, ain't it? That uniform?"

The man sighed deeply, but then did finally surrender up his hand for shaking. Ben shook. He had sympathy for all such persons who could not themselves be postmen, and must be satisfied with administering tests.

He gathered his children, plucking one of them out of the crowd and the other from the pool and then, with his wife, aimed straight for the dry goods store where he had once spent so much time among products and items that he had never been able to afford himself. Today it was

Wooley's boy in attendance, an illiterate, (as Ben happened to know), with straw instead of hair.

"Well, reckon as how I'm going to be a postman now," said Ben, (the boy gaped), "and so I figure I'd better 'stock up,' don't you know—buy things—while I'm here."

The boy nodded. His attention, however, was upon Ben's two sons, one of them bleeding upon the bolts of cloth. Betty had gotten into a velvety material of some kind, a dark stuff nappier than a lamb's fleece. With such a salary as Ben now had in prospect, he saw no reason why he could not buy a number of things. Of course, the clerk could not be everywhere. He chose therefore to stand with the eldest boy, using a handkerchief to staunch his bloodied head.

Twenty-five

So Ben—his life was half-gone when he became a government man. Too early, he rose, (he had had no sleep, none), and went into the next room to get into his uniform. Was it to be his fate on this his first day to lose directions and end up disgracing himself, the government, and all those hungering for their mail? The thought made him tremble—he had a headache—not for the life of him could he get his tunic straight. Finally, he came out.

"Oh!" said his wife. "Look at all them buttons!"

"*We* didn't have buttons. Never needed 'em!"

Quickly the speller drained off two cups of coffee and went outside. It was a clear day, with brightness in the fields. He would have given anything *now* for his well-remembered mule of '92, and to have *him* in place of this modern horse whom Betty had so fopped-up with red ribbons for its braided mane. Now, finishing off the coffee, Ben climbed aboard the buggy and began to adjust the reins.

The first quarter-mile went well—he did it with dignity. However, it carried him only from the house to the highway, a short distance. Perhaps he ought rather to be standing in front of his classroom once more, and once more going through the spelling as in old times. He did so miss it, spelling and reading and all that "life of the mind." His horse, certainly, had no mind—Ben must know the entire route by himself, and much else besides.

He moved on at a trot, past Mitchell's place, past a low-lying area still under flood, and past the plantation house, ruined now, and so full with Negro families that the walls were bulging. One man indeed, a stranger to Ben, was sunning himself on one of the fallen columns. As to how these people had come into such good holdings, land that was friable and aromatic too . . . Ben could not imagine. In any case, they had no mail, nor did he care to be seen associating too closely with them. Yes, he nodded to Burb, to Placenta, and nodded to Vee too, who looked to be pregnant again. Was this again her brother's doing? Ben clucked to the horse, urging her forward. Truth was, he was embarrassed by his own popularity in these parts. Nor did he wish to be asked for one more "loan."

That was when he made the first mistake in his career, permitting his horse to get tangled up in a drove of pigs being ushered across the road by two young boys who saluted and began, both of them, muttering gibberish at him. It was rare that Ben should make *two* errors in such rapid succession; nevertheless, he now did take out something, a few half-cent pieces, and then handed them over, knowing full well that he was being outrageously mulcted in order that the road might clear.

In truth, he did not understand these people. *Their* land was better than his; why then did their homes stand in such awful need of repair? *His* home never needed repair, nor would he have allowed it to have such needs, never, not even if he had had to work through the night, night after night, working by candlelight with a bad liver and Jasper.

It cost him two cents; finally he sprang free. Home was far behind, his horse losing zest, and still he had not yet delivered his first piece of mail. Indeed, he had more mail than before, considering that he had been given a peck of sweet potatoes to be carried forward to a "cousin" a little further down the road.

The next mile went quickly; he began spelling words out loud. With his uniform, it seemed to him that speed itself had dignity to it. He ran past a field of lush brown cows, each cow facing off in the direction of its own choosing. Suddenly, Ben drew up abruptly, and then forced the horse to go back a few paces. Here was likely the most beautiful scenery he had seen in his life, a blue furze against an endlessly changing sky that made it seem as if the Deity Himself were going through a rehearsal of all His moods. Behind were hills, fogs lifting from the summits, and further still, a cleared space where one of the innumerable hermits of the region had established himself in a cone-shaped hut.

Ben took out his map and marked the spot and then also got down and set up a memorial of stones alongside the route. No doubt about it, he was growing more and more susceptible to beauty, to landscape, and to this special strain of imported cattle that fed so abundantly on flowers that they too, day by day, were changing into colors. He was trying to force the horse back yet further, hoping for an even better view, when he descried a forlorn-looking countrywoman who had hiked all the distance down to the highway and now was waiting with downcast eyes upon her mail.

Ben lifted his hat to her. Without intending, she had loosed some hundred ducks upon him, wherefore he must *again* wait for the path to clear. He had neglected to hand over all her mail, (three pieces, together with a catalog from Cincinnati—it was his third error thus far). He stopped, got down, and carried it back to her in person. He would not, however, deliver it direct into her cupped hands, not when the law required that it go straight into the box. *This* then was the dignity of it, namely that she might, or might not, read it, and might, or might not, find it good—it was no affair of his.

He drove on. He had come down into a swampy stretch where the highway was overhung with clots of Spanish moss that dangled from the branches. It was an evil district, with no agricultural promise to it whatsoever. He hoped to get through it quickly, until he recalled that it was precisely here that his uncle dwelled, a man named Mordecai, called also "Bender of Pines."

Ben drove on hurriedly, passing over the frail bridge that had been designed, so it seemed, to entice automobiles and cars. It was frailer than it looked. The man's house was itself in ruins, part of the roof absent, and fitted with a door that covered not much more than half the actual opening. Through this space, wolves and swine could have entered at freedom, had they not known what sort of man it was inside. Ben knocked courteously and then, getting no reply, entered with caution.

Mordecai lived in nuisance and filth. Having never had a wife, he lay now, eyes open, a look of wonder on his face.

"Howdy!" quoth Ben.

The man smiled. And that was when he perceived Ben's uniform, which caused him suddenly to sit upright.

"Gone for a soldier! I'm proud of you, boy."

"No, no; I'm the mail carrier now."

"Wal!"

"But I don't have nothing for you today."

"Hit don't matter." He was a rangy man, big-jointed, a

tobacco chewer, and had been known to sleep for such
long periods as that all his strength, which was famous,
had been preserved. In the district of the cabin, all exist-
ing trees had been broken off long before, and used for
firewood.

"How's Eddie?"

"Dead."

"You don't tell! Wal!"

"Long time ago."

"You don't tell." (And now Ben saw that he would not
be getting out of bed after all.) "Who's tending the 'altar'?"

They laughed, both.

"Got me a wife now," Ben said.

"No!"

"It's the truth. Got me a farm too."

"Got him a farm." The man turned slowly, adjusting
the grain sack that he used for a pillow. Beneath the bed,
Ben saw how the chamber pot was full, and more than
full.

"Well, reckon I'd better pro-ceed. The government,
don't you know."

"I suppose. Now you tell him come see me, hear?"

"He's dead."

"And tell him to bring them three dollars too."

Ben went out. He seemed to remember a barn here,
and other buildings; now, no stick remained. Even his
own horse, hunting for chestnuts, had ambled off some
fifty rods or more, forcing Ben to chase her down. It was
absolutely amazing to Ben, that whereas he had not been
absent a full five minutes, yet the sweet potatoes were
gone.

Here in this southern part of the county, there were
reptiles in great quantity, but especially a newly-evolved
species of "ground crabs," (so-called), that had lined up

shoulder to shoulder alongside the road while displaying their claws on high. Ben drove on, paying little regard to them. As it happened, one of the letters in his pouch bore a foreign stamp, one so beautiful and well-engraven that it portrayed a sixteenth-century sailing vessel becalmed in a blood-red sea—it was this that chiefly occupied his thoughts when, suddenly, the rain began to come down.

His buggy did have a hood to it; unfortunately, the hood had leaks. Now, his hat pulled low, he drew off onto the side of the road and once again inspected the stamp. No further doubt, there *were* a certain number of little men standing on deck, and at least one of them was pointing off to something or another, the source of all their troubles, (was it a whale? dreadful weather coming in?), that lay several inches off the stamp itself, and thus was invisible to Ben. He was dreaming. Few things in life he loved more than the noise of rain upon a roof. Ahead, he saw hills, smoke leaping from the summits, and behind him dunes in which the crabs were scrambling for cover. Perhaps he had been unjust—the mare was working loyally, dancing through the puddles with her peculiar grin. Suddenly, he almost ran into another buggy coming on straight toward him. Ben called, quite uselessly. The driver was a stern-looking person reading in a Bible—Ben knew well these types of extreme religion— who passed by quickly without so much as a nod.

In any case, the time had come to take up his lunch, to cut the string, and to see what his wife had done for him. Chicken! He would have recognized her work anywhere. Well-sprinkled with pepper, the three pages of meat reclined upon a bun cushioned with lettuce, tomatoes, and cheese. The pickles he had made himself, green as gars and warted from head to toe; they derived out of his own personal garden. And as if all this were not enough, the woman had also supplied him with a jar of very black coffee as well. Ben ate everything, he did, all save the coffee. The coffee he drank.

The volcanoes stood just in front, and yet he seemed to have come no closer to them than of an hour ago. That he was dangerously near to the county boundary, he knew it from a thousand indications, and from other clues as well. Someone, he saw, had begun to lay out a field, even going so far as to extract most of the stumps, but only then to give it up and run off and leave it. Considering the rain, the chill, and the smell of burning pine, it seemed to him that it might almost be October now. And that was when he saw from whence the smoke was issuing—a queer-looking little cottage built entirely from pine cones and sweet gum balls, and with a roof bending under its burden of honeysuckle and vines.

Ben dismounted and moved toward it, towing the horse and buggy after him. Itself, the chimney was tall and spindly—he kept well clear of it—and, apparently, put together out of bits of broken jars and bottles.

"Howdy!" he said, drawing near to the figure in the window.

"You bring them 'taters?"

"Reckon I lost 'em."

He heard a groan, and then also two others groaning from deep within. Then:

"Hey! You ain't Dwayne!"

"I'm the *new* carrier." (He could not help but peep inside, even to putting his head through the opening. It was the oddest of buildings, and so much more spacious and comfortable than he would have supposed.)

"Well I'll be . . . ! Well hell, you might as well come on in now."

"Hell," said the woman. "He *is* in."

It was a peculiarly-fashioned doorway, made more for mice than for a full-grown man. He had to stoop low.

"I'm your new carrier," he announced, doffing his cap. "Now if there's ever anything I can do . . ."

"Just 'taters."

A boy ran up, bringing a drink. It surprised him, first, to find that it was liquor, and then secondly, to find it served out of a gourd. The other children, soiled ones, stood shyly in the corner.

"Three!" said Ben. "No, *four*. How many children do you have then? Altogether, I mean?"

"Children? Now don't go thinking them's is *ours*."

"No, no." There were dogs too; one indeed had climbed up into Ben's lap and gone promptly to sleep. Ben was tired as well; never had he been able to stand up against rain and warmth and liquor, especially not so when he had gone a full night without sleep.

When he woke, and when he saw that a certain time had gone by, then he ran outside and leapt to horse and buggy. Soon enough, the sun would vanish, something that was happening more and more frequently as the century, previously so young, as it wore on. Ben began to feel old. So many generations had come and gone while leaving behind such inconsiderable memorials to themselves—here a silo and there a barn, and across the road a corn field in which someone had labored himself to death, but which now was growing up in scrub once more. A windmill came up, a giant, as it were, who had fallen into bad times, and had something broken in its head.

He went racing on in silence, never allowing himself, not even once, the horse neither, to step over the county line. That he was in the precise middle of his route, and that the moment happened also to coincide with the exact mid-point in his life. . . Of this, he knew nothing. He did see that he had encroached into the township called *Leprean*, the prettiest in the county. And anyway, he loved all towns and provinces whose names were in "L."

He worked for two hours more, passing out the stuff
to the women and farmers and to the children who came
racing to gaze upon the new postman. Finally, an old
man, one of the same generation as Jasper, stepped out
in front and hindered him from going further.
"You ain't fixing to go through the 'hollow'?"
Ben had to suppose that in fact he *was* so fixing.
"I wouldn't! 'Course now, I ain't you."
"Is there any other way?"
The man pondered for a long time, thinking about it,
until his mind began to drift. Ben asked:
"What's down there then, that I shouldn't ought to
go?"
"What's down there? What's down there? I'll tell you
what's down there!"
"Good."
"Why do you reckon Dwayne quit?"
"You mean . . . ?" (He pointed to the hollow.)
"Shore!" (The old man pointed too.)
"Aw shoot, I've heard all them old stories."
"That don't mean they ain't true."
"About how a bunch of unionists, along with certain
Negroes . . ."
"That's exactly right."
". . . whom, having freed, they enslaved . . ."
The man looked at him and then, suddenly, shrugged,
turned, and walked away. The speller was left to admire
the old man's farm, a green sward of width and depth, all
of it touched off by a four-acre pond with swans wearing
mascara and burnished bills; even the old one also kept
twisting to gaze back at the sight of it. And all this time,
the day itself was darkening, with streaks running down
the hill. Now in truth did he begin to regret his too-
lengthy nap. He even thought of putting aside his last

twenty pieces and of delivering them instead on the day following, something his better self absolutely forbade. In any case, he still had the foreign letter with its gorgeous stamp. Would the addressee allow him to see what it held inside? It was that moment that a coyote leapt up out of the weeds and dashed across in front of him, turning at the last instant to expose a face so full of loathing and actual hatred for all men that Ben was stunned and shocked, and perhaps even a little intimidated by it too. The mare was too demoralized to care.

Spanish moss everywhere. He saw persimmon trees, kumquats, scuppernongs, and muscadine, enough here to sustain any number of Pennsylvanian Unionist footpads and all their associated trash for as long as they might want. Better he had brought his shotgun; instead, now, he removed the quirt from its socket and laid it across his lap. The boxes were further and further apart, some of them without any apparent connection to any house that *he* could see. Night was coming in quickly now. But it was only after he had rounded the bend and found three men in the road that his consternation grew serious. One was young, one black, and one looked like he might well be a leftover from '64. Ben reached for, but could not find, the shotgun that he should have brought.

"Howdy!"

"You're late."

"Shut up," said the old one. "Just shut up! Are you going to?"

"Got any money?"

"Money! No, no. I got . . ." (He had started to say 'sweet potatoes.') Then "Hey! that was a pretty good rain we had."

"Alright, keep your goddamn money; we don't want it anyhow. Just give us that there 'mail,' and you'll be alright. Now *that's* fair, ain't it?"

"I reckon not. The government, don't you know.

Rules, rules." (The young one, Ben realized, was not normal, and meanwhile the old one kept his eye all times upon the uniform.)

"Now just what regiment was you *in*, exactly?"

"Hell, we could take the horse. Hell, that ought to be worth something."

"I asked him what regiment, and I asked him kindly too."

"You crave that uniform? Hell, *I'll* get it for you."

The young one came closer. Ben saw a hand coming for him that had but three fingers on it; he now understood more clearly why Dwayne had quit.

"I'll have that uniform."

"Yes, I'd like to let you have it. But . . ."

"What did he say?"

"He said he'd *like* to, but . . ."

"But I can't."

"'Can't'?"

"The government." Now Ben lifted the quirt and used it, using it not on the man but on the horse, who lurched and ran. It took them all by surprise, saving only the veteran himself, than whom *nothing* probably could surprise. Ben heard him say: "He's leaving," saying it calmly, and then saying: "He's gone."

Ahead was open space. The sun was gone, down, finished, out of sight and deleted from memory. He had but some half-dozen pieces of mail still remaining, and for this the government wanted him to ride for miles and miles and even, at one point, to dip down into the next county. Now, almost before he was aware of it, he found himself in a tiny village that he had never known existed, and in which all the people had come down in a group in order to receive him.

All his life he had wanted it thus, to be greeted in this fashion. A cheer went up, he saw hands stretched toward him, whereupon he actually reached out and shook one of them, before he realized that it was simply groping for mail.

"Where's Dwayne?"

"Say, how'd you get past them Pennsylvania fellows?"

"Didn't bring nothing to *eat*, did you?"

"Got any money?"

Ben grew confused. He had lost his hat in the melee, and now he saw that one of the little boys was wearing it. A haggard-looking woman was suggesting he stay the night. Finally, his confusion growing, (and it seemed to him that he had no other real choice), he used the quirt again.

The village had a gate; it hung by a single hinge. Beyond, it was all alluvial chert with pines on one side and sown land on the other. He hurried through a field of wild roses that, in the night, resembled so many little hearts swaying on stems. Now that it was midnight, this whole region had an evil cast.

He did have the presence to feed his horse, offering up a double ration of such good oats that Ben began to envy her. He used this interval for setting up his lantern and fixing it aloft, and then for rolling a cigarette and smoking it down. Finally, he set out across what looked, if not indeed like a sea, like a bay at least, assuming that bays looked like this.

He cast a meager beam. He saw great blunt leviathans coming up for air, knowing full well they were merely little hills of a particular shape. That he was close to drifting off into pure imagination, he knew it for a certainty when he passed by a certain well-known termite column called "Lot's Wife," a much-weathered landmark worn down by now to a mere nub of salt of which it was impossible to say in which direction the woman had originally been facing at the time. He was thinking about this, and about the sole remaining letter in his satchel, when suddenly he splashed into a hoard of broken pottery shards that made a noise like that of glass. And like glass too, he assumed it must be bad upon the horse's feet. This was by far the most primitive corner of the county, with no prominent feature to it other than these dozens of antique clay "igloos," all of them long ago broken apart and long ago robbed. It further disconcerted him to see outbreaks of phosphorous here and there, as if the desert were strewn with eyes. And that, of course, was the very moment when he *saw*, (for he was too far away to *hear*), where one of the Birmingham iron foundries had just exploded.

It was late indeed when finally he penetrated to that extreme region, hitherto seen by him only on a map. Here, he thought that he could catch the first faint smell of winter from afar, putting him in mind of his spelling days, of harvest time, and of the frozen frost that soon enough must again be materializing in the hills. Crude was his vehicle, himself unadvanced, winter coming in, and yet he had traveled a very great distance on this night. Here now was that house (a light glowing in an upstairs window) that had cost him so much effort, and where too he must surrender the letter with the lovely stamp. It was when he looked back and saw a girl (quite barefooted), saw her come racing out and take the letter and, bestowing kisses on it, saw her turn and go racing back . . . He could not but laugh at loud.

He came in at a good clip, prancing past Wooley's house, past the broken-down cabins of Vee and Burb, and then past Oldenfield's acres crowded with what once were believed to be scarecrows, until it was learned that his house too was full of them, all of them wearing his dead wife's clothes. Never had the speller experienced such pride, knowing that on this his first day he had deserved well, and knowing that now he had a salary. He had left home early, whereas now, looking at the window, he saw his own wife holding up a baby that, apparently, had come into being during the time that he himself had been away.

Twenty-six

What manner of things, objects and wealth, children and tools, what sort of items did he possess at age forty-two? Of children he had six, or rather five, not to include the one who came last week. Oftentimes he saw them at their doings. And oftentimes indeed he saw them from afar!

First, his buildings, four of these, he had built them all himself. The house that used to be a barn, should it be counted as barn or as a home? Or, should he perhaps count the corn crib first? Instead, he strode straight to the smokehouse, and the vision of the two smoked hogs that warranted how no one would be starving *this* autumn on land that was his, no, nor during the hard winter months neither.

He did have a barn; he did not, however, go to it. Instead, he returned to the smokehouse again and checked the latch.

He had a cotton bin, and in it, cotton. Cotton it was, therefore tasteless; he could not conceive how civilization had learned to make use of such stuff. How much did he have? The better part of a bale. And who had reaped it for him? Reapers three.

Truth was, he could not distinctly remember how he had come into so much wealth. Hard by was the barn— he went to it now—the very citadel, as it were, of his holdings. His inclination was to climb into the loft, which in fact he did, but only to uncover the tiny Buford, the least of his boys, who had gotten there before him and was drinking the molasses straight from the jar. Ben saw it all, everything, and recognized at once that the child had been vomiting on himself.

"What the plague!" (said Ben.) "Well, I'll be jiggered!"

The boy leapt up, running for the ladder, even though he was too drunk to get to it. Sometimes Ben wanted to laugh at him, and sometimes he got mad. As to the boy himself, he was as yet too small, too vomit-bespattered for Ben to foresee just what his essential quality might turn out to be.

Ben came down. The girl "Ralinda," his "firstling," as he called her, (for she had come into being during Ben's first year of landownership), Ralinda was in the yard. He could read her well, this one, and knew her essential quality too. She *never* wanted to work, and today she was especially sullen about having been asked to milk the cow.

"Lands!" said Ben. "Ain't you finished *yet*?"

Sullen she was. Moreover, she dressed like an old woman and would never marry. Buford had disappeared. It *was* a bright day nevertheless, cheerful above and cheerful in the woods, and many bright clouds reflecting in the well. Years had gone by; Ben now knew how to do his route in under five hours, and still be home in time to plow.

He had built for himself a "store," famous in the locality, where he sold tobacco to the white people, and sardines to the black. It was his third-eldest who loved to sit behind the counter, to accept the money and chide the Negroes and arrange the wares. Ben called to her now, whereon she grinned and held up the morning's profits for him to see—three blackened coins as big as pies. This one *would* marry, a good proprietress, and a speller too.

All in all, it was a bright day, even biblical in its depiction of life upon the farm. He moved on, perhaps another twenty yards, going more and more slowly, pondering about it, and then finally stopping when it occurred to him that this might probably be the second-best day he was ever to have. And to think that it had come so unexpectedly, a gift from out of nowhere—he snorted and shook his head—and at a time when he was already forty-eight! Came now the dog, wearing flour on his nose. Ben was close to joy; he had six peach trees, and bees in every bloom. The world itself was sparkling, bathed in light; suddenly, he clapped hands and spun around, that is to say until he saw his second-eldest watching darkly. Further, he spied the woman who had brought him his lands; at once, the idea formed in his head of going forward silently and then of jumping out upon her when she least expected it.

Which possessions had he, what books, which numbers of bees? Nine books—he went right inside to count them now. The bees, the bees were past counting, nor would they stand still long enough for being counted. His *Agricultural Yearbook!*—the simple truth of it was that he had kept the thing, and not at all returned it to its genuine owner. All this, books, money, a few foreign stamps, he kept all of it in the bottom drawer along with the few fragments of antique pottery taken on his route. But of money, he had nearly a thousand dollars now, along with certain small reserves in the smokehouse.

Jasper too had a room of his own, although Ben preferred not to visit there anymore. The old man had held on to his smithing tools, the false arm, and in the corner a heap of rotting leather that might once have comprised a harness. Furthermore, he had taken recently to spitting his black juice out the window, and of missing.

In the kitchen, Ben and his wife owned a set of cutlery made of tin, also a dozen drinking glasses with, each of them, the picture of a corn flower on it. He took one now, something he did very seldom, and poured himself half an inch of spirituous liquor, brown and sweet. This was the best seat in his whole demesne, with a view that flew straight down the lane, across the road, and smashed into the woods.

It was quiet, bright, life itself more placid today than in a cow's eye. The noonday sun had bestowed a patch of light on the floor that seemed to be crawling with worms. These worms, he saw, were dragging the patch toward the door. It *was* warm. And yet, to his certain knowledge, it had never yet been as warm as he would have liked, nor as placid as he wanted.

At two o'clock, he headed for the bee glade, but only to turn and come back home again when he saw how testy they had become. No doubt about it, they had been mixing with strays. And indeed, Ben had burned them out long ago, were it not that his children were addicted to the honey.

He turned west, toward the dry acres that marched with Mitchell's. It was littered here with pebbles and stone; he could have built whole buildings from the stuff at hand, if only he had enough bonding material. (The urge to raise up an "altar," or "needle"—he was still far from that.) In fact, these were the least of his acres, with no usefulness whatsoever to them save that it was here that Jasper like to retreat when in his religious moods.

Ben stopped. He realized there was a long black millipede riding precisely on the toe of his boot. Carefully the speller brought it up for a more detailed examination and then, taking off his glasses, brought it closer still. No, he simply did not understand such things—he never would— nor could he imagine how it felt to be like one of these. Just then, without wishing, he dropped the animal, whereupon it instantaneously resolved itself into ten roistering centipedes who scrambled off at once in all directions.

He went on, the postman, until he touched the boundary where, as often as not, (but not today), Mitchell would be waiting with his shotgun. Himself, Ben had no envy to set foot on territory that was not his own. It was a clear day, blue above and blue below, many white moths and night still 4,000 miles away. Suddenly, intrigued by what he saw, he halted and began to dig out an old-fashioned medicine bottle with a glass cork in it. This day had contained many surprises, but none so surprising as this—to find what looked like a tiny scroll inside tied up in faded ribbon. He knew, of course, based upon his geological readings, how this whole county had once been covered in seas, and knew too how the Ancient Creeks had used manifold methods for communicating over broad distances, one with another. Again, he held up the bottle to the sun. Never yet had he peeped at someone else's mail, not in all his years upon the route. He smoked, sat, fidgeted and, still holding the jar up to the light, continued trying to decipher through the clouded glass what looked to him like a very queer sort of writing indeed.

It required all the best that was in him. Finally, most reluctantly, he returned the jar to its place and sprinkled dirt over it. *He'd* not be the one to open it, though he knew the size and feel of temptation, when temptation stared him in the face.

It was while he was dealing with it, (sprinkling the dirt), that he spied his wife floating past quietly with the basket on her arm. Quickly Ben got to his feet and began to follow. Not that she imagined she was alone! On the contrary, he caught her glancing back nervously, and then go speeding forward even faster than before. He would have recognized that bonnet anywhere. Suddenly, she darted off into the grove.

The dog barked, a deer ran past; his immediate

thought was that she had taken on this form in order to escape. It was not easy, pursuing her through the reeds that she knew so much better than did he. It was the bonnet that gave her away. Finally he caught her in an empty zone, with no place to hide. She edged backwards, half in fear, half in delight. Ben spoke first:

"I knowed you was down here."

"Well I don't wonder! And I knowed you was chasing me too." (She had backed to the edge of the woods, looking for an opening.)

"You know what's fixing to happen, don't you?"

She nodded. Suddenly Ben grabbed for the basket. What things did he see, which fruits, whose apples and nuts? In fact there were more of quail eggs than anything else. The woman herself had come to a stop against a tree, wherefore if he wanted to embrace either, he must perforce embrace both.

"It's happening now, ain't it?"

Ben nodded. She was strong, she was not strong enough. He had seen this before: lift her off the earth and she lost what strength she had.

What tools had he, which seeds, whose weapons and awls? How many vials of clarified calomel with bright labels? He saw little Buford move past, vomit-besmirched, dragging on the dog. Certainly the day was failing; it caused the corn in the field to fold its arms. He did love his Sundays, but now Sunday was over.

Twenty-seven

The clay-colored sun had arisen an hour ago. He measured, Ben did, finding that it had climbed barely six inches into the sky. Ben looked again, blushing, and having then to admit that in fact this was still the moon.

Once more he found himself hunched-up in the buggy, once more waiting upon the authentic sun before he dared to go onto the highway among motorized cars. Itself, his coat was black, his shoes quite bright, the hat wide-brimmed; nor could he fail to observe how Mitchell was waiting upon the sun in mere dungarees.

Sometimes it did seem to Ben that he was trotting, not through any *real* landscape at all, but rather passing in and out of the rather dreamy imaginings of a giant who liked to lie for long hours, smiling, in fields of corn. Accordingly therefore, today's landscape was highly wrinkled, yellow in hue, and dark about the edges. He passed two mules dressed in the same velvet (now much the worse for wear) that they had been born in, both of them exposing long sorrowful faces that reminded the speller of a certain postman he had known one time. The barn too looked to be sorrowing, owing to the placement of the mouth and eyes, and where its excessive brains of hay were tumbling out.

Below, the terrain turned flat. To Ben it indicated that the giant had snoozed off again and was dreaming smooth dreams. He passed the Methodist spire, the Baptist steeple, and finally the hollow belfry of the *New Last Chance Reformed Assembly*. It did excite him—he couldn't help it—to come riding into town at holiday when the square was full. There was more dignity to it, in looking straight ahead, far more so than in acknowledging the drinkers and louts that clustered in front of the hotel and called to him by name. Much had changed since his dry goods days—he had to ride three times all around the square before he could find a filling station and an available gas pump, where he could tether the mare.

First things first: He required *seed*, wanted to purchase *feed*, went behind the livery and *peed*. At one time, he had enjoyed the respect of every dog in town; now, a small black-and-white yapper was striking at his ankle. He had been away too long, had forgotten city methods. There seemed to him too many faces, each thinking too many thoughts. Suddenly, he turned away to hide his own face. Hattie was coming.

He wanted to flee. That ever in this world he had had to do with such a one, and no matter how rich she now obviously was . . . In fact, they passed without speaking. Ben found it all the more awkward in that he was carrying a stack of honey boxes, some of them leaking onto his clothes. Quickly he turned off into the grocery. The man, however, had seen him coming.

"Howdy!"

"B. R."

"I brung you some more honey—it's good!—want some? Shoot, I'm only asking twenty cents the box."

"We don't get much call for honey, B. R."

"What?"

"Well hell. It stands to reason, Ben! I mean if you're going to *give* it away all the time, why then nobody's going to *buy* any."

"I see."

"Now don't go getting mad at *me*. Alright, here, let me have one box then."

"No, no, I don't want your money, not if it's just *one* you want. No, I wouldn't charge you for just one."

The man sighed, but then did take the box and put it under the counter.

"You see, it's not just honey, Boland. No, I've got my route, got the crops, got the hens."

"We know that, Ben."

"So I ain't going to *starve* exactly."

"Nobody wants you to starve."

"Got Jasper. And squirrels! My boy brings home two or three of them every day. *Almost* every day."

"It's a fine thing—boys."

"Peaches!"

"You bet. Oh, you're fixed up real good out there, Ben; everybody knows that."

"So I don't just have to *sell* my honey, you understand. No, I can give it away whenever I want. And *whoever* I want, too."

"That's the truth." Then: "How's Betty these days?"

"So I'll just leave all this honey, *clover* honey, with you, Boland, and shoot, you can sell in on *consignment*, as the fellow says. Understand what I mean?"

"No, no. No, Ben, I . . . Hey! Why not try Cecil? He's always been kind of . . . Try Cecil."

They parted on good terms. Cecil's was closed however, and meanwhile the honey was leaking. Ben went on. He was thinking seriously of turning in at the barber's for a professional haircut with oils; instead, that moment, Abner strolled up.

"B. R. hisself."

"Howdy, Ab."

"Old B. R. Tell me, B. R., how's that kidney business of yours doing *now*, huh?" He grinned.

"Hurts."

"Old B. R. and his honey. Ain't nobody going to buy any of that shit."

Ben looked off. "Are you still teaching, Ab?"

"Well hell yes I'm still teaching. What, did you think I was like you? Run off and leave a job?"

"I saw Hattie."

"Hattie's married now."

"No!"

"Married to me. And I don't want to hear no more about it neither."

"No, no."

"Memnon's dead, who used to run errands. Grady too."

"No!"

"Got hisself kilt in a knife fight. Oh he was a bad one. Shem, he's dead too."

"Can't be!"

"Is. Got into some bad honey, is what I heard. And what about you, B. R., what with all that land of yours? I don't reckon you got time anymore for all that reading and whatnot."

"I *am* busy, sure am. Jasper helps some."

"Jas . . . ! Why I figured that old son-of-a-bitch was *dead* by now. Should be."

They parted on reasonable terms. Ben saw, (but did not speak to), Shem, who was by no means dead, and who had never purchased even one box of Benjamin's honey. Dagon's place was busy, some of the Negroes going inside and coming back out, and then milling about on the porch as if they were actual white men. And that was when Ben laid eyes for the first time upon the bus that had been modified into a traveling library and now was parked in front of the store itself.

Ben ran.

What titles did he find? Which authors? What colors were the books? Blue, many of them, but also one very fat one that was green. Even by his standards crude, it had a map in it that purported to show the Antique World as it then stood. He could not but laugh, knowing as he did that Asia was considerably larger than that, and moreover was usually colored yellow in token of the people who had chosen to dwell there. His temptation was to take the thing and be off with it; instead, he "checked it out," signing his full name. Once outside, he discovered that he could not very well walk, read, wave to the people he knew, and keep the honey from leaking into the book all at the same time. And yet, he was aware of the sound of classes going on in that same courthouse where he too used to teach. He stopped, turned, came to the window and then, taking out his handkerchief, spread it on the ground and rested the book on it, he himself stepping onto the book.

It was years, years and years, years later and the man himself long ago dead and gone when his second-eldest's son first heard about it—how that the whole class had turned to find a "horrible apparition" in the window, in fact a face, the face of a speller, a speller's face pressing at the glass.

Twenty-eight

He was disappointed. After a full day's work, he had expected to sleep and sleep well; instead, his mind was churning out the usual "butter" of old forbidden thoughts and partly-remembered places. His liver hurt. Now finally he rose up on one elbow in order to look more closely at his wife. What, really, did he know of women? Just this—that this one had *wanted* to be put to use from the beginning. And a good thing too, since he had wanted to do the using. As for going in unto a woman and begetting little boys and girls on her . . . He had needed no books nor agricultural bulletins whatsoever. Ben came closer. She had developed little creases just here under her eye where, however, he couldn't touch them unless he wished to endanger her sleep.

He got up and moved about the house. In the forest, an owl was blaring in tedious repertoire, shortly to be spelled by the nightingales of three o'clock. Even at this hour the house was full of the sound of shrinking joists, of an old man snoring, and of two young women, daughters of his, sleeping the sleep slept by sleepers. He was 54 now, no longer just 40, and had numerous dead brothers planted in various parts about the county. It had made him heir to an obelisk that, the last time he saw it, had broken into pieces, and the pieces lying in tall grass.

Moderate was the night, and long shadows with fingers on them. There was nothing else in the world like this—a crepuscule so sweet that the farmers could do their plowing, as it were, in ambergris, easy on the knife. Never had Ben bought into the philosophy that nightly appearances are to be considered less valid than those of day. On *this* night, the whole world looked like one walled town, with vines crawling up the parapets. He heard a swine grunting, a door slam, a radio. No further doubt about it—there *were* Negroes living in the draw on land that was theoretically his alone. Ben came closer. He was expecting nightingales at any moment; what he got, of course, was one lone whippoorwill calling weakly from poor Hubert's place.

He was thinking, talking, smoking, and strolling when Betty came up. They had had no "romance," remember, properly speaking.

"I woke," (she said), "but you were not there!"

"Nay, all's well. Nay, hie thee back to bed, dear, for all goes well." (Actually, he said: "Howdy.")

"And be it the route as frets thee?"

Ben blushed. Down below, the swine had given over and gone to bed. Indeed, apart from Hubert's place, the whole county had lapsed to silence.

"Ain't it something?" she said. "Why, that kudzu looks just like some old *castle*, don't it? And that moon! I declare."

"You understand we still got to pay off them debts, you understand that, don't you?"

"Oh! We have the eggs."

"Now if we sold off some of this *timber*. . ."

"And the cow—we have *her*."

"Or find some work in town. You could do it if anybody can!"

(No. Married now and middle-aged, she declined to

set foot on land that was not her own.) "No, I have so many hens now."

Ben groaned. They had come to an elevation where the pines were bent and whence they could see the whole distance to town and back. He counted four burning lamps, or rather five, or four rather that were consistent and another that seemed to be sputtering out in a hasty code. It was all so strange, the magic of distances. If he set out *now*, why then soon he could be *there*.

"Looks like John James is still awake."

Ben knew him, knew his hovel, and knew further how since his sickness he had taken to shooting other people's cows.

"See how narrow the village, constrained, and how it strings out along the river. And then too, the enormous immensity of the woods themselves."

She stood, gaping at it. Ben could not see whether it be her regular night cap she was wearing, or if she had gotten into her daytime bonnet.

"And if some night you wake to find me gone, and if some night you find no lights at all . . . Well! That will prove how the village too has disappeared, "eaten," as it were, by cruel Time and history."

It troubled her. Nevertheless, she was in habit of believing what he said. Ben went on:

"Oh yes. And no one then will be able to say where once we had a farm."

"On account of the woods?"

"Woods, yes. Avalanches and whatnot. And Time itself."

"But what about the *house*?"

"Well! It ain't reasonable to think our place will make out any better than other folks' places."

"No better?"

"Nope. Why someday this whole field will be covered over in weeds again, and trees sprouting up. Oh, you can depend upon that."

"And how about the children? How about Buford?"

"Dead. Oh yes, you can depend on that too."

"Well my lands! Then who's going to take care of this here farm then?"

"It won't be a 'farm.' There won't be any 'farm.'"

"Well now that's just hooey! I ain't going to listen to you no more. Why, I never heard the like of it!"

She might well be upset, and yet he could not fail to see that she continued to cling tightly to his arm. Far off, two counties away, a dull faint glow leapt up briefly where the last of the volcanoes were smoldering palely. Itself, the night was cool however, and made the woman shiver. And when they looked again, there were two lights only, not four, both feeble, and the moon in dark phase.

Twenty-nine

It came time for the 1927 Birmingham Mail Carriers Convention of 1927. Ben rose early and got into his best clothes. And that was when it came down on him that of all the things that he had never done, yet he *would* nevertheless have attended the 1927 Birmingham Mail Carriers Convention of that same year.

An hour later, he found himself in a car alongside some four or five others of his profession, some of whom he knew and some not, and one whom he respected and three he respected not at all. He was a formal man, Benjamin, and preferred to sit in dignity looking straight ahead. His colleagues, *they* of course were laughing and drinking, (drinking in the morning), and talking of Negroes, of money, and, with voices low, of women themselves. Apparently they intended to behave very badly, just as soon as they hit town. Meanwhile, three of them were snickering at *him*. It is true that he was wearing

Jasper's hat, true too that he had brought his meals with him, including two quarts of milk.

"Old B. R.! We're going to have us some *fun*, ain't that right?"

"Shoot."

"What, you don't like fun?"

In truth, he didn't. He knew what it would come down to, namely how they would be wanting to go in unto a woman, or something in that line.

"Shoot. No sir, I just want to get one look at that *ocean*, that's all."

They laughed, laughed uproariously, and only now did it fall in upon Ben that there was not likely to be much ocean in Birmingham. Nor was he enthusiastic about the smell and the sensation of being shut up in an iron car that went forward of itself. Ben sighed. How much longer, how, before this vogue would pass?

And yet . . . Certainly he *was* seeing a great amount on this day. It astounded him how that the country was so much larger than he had been led to believe, longer too, flatter, higher, lower, together with farms and domiciles more noble than he would have thought possible. The wealth of it! How *could* he have so wasted his own life? Pastures he saw, grass in them as green as paint, also a two-story house that could have held a family of twenty, assuming the world had twenty people as lucky as that. He saw a small goat operation that looked to do doing very well, with goats of several generations mixing freely. Even here, he saw certain possible improvements—a fence, a roof. He yearned to stop, get out, do the job himself and make all things perfect. His own life had been wasted. And then too, his spirits darkened when he caught a glimpse of the obsolete western hills beyond which, according to the reports that came to him, a certain diminution had been verified along the Edge.

They came bouncing up over a rising just in time for the speller to descry what was unquestionably the tallest and at the same time the most perilous building that he had ever seen. But mostly it was the architect himself— had no one been willing to tell the man about high winds? (Ben knew from experience what had happened to his father's tower, now lying only partly in Calauria, and partly elsewhere.) He was thinking on this when, suddenly, he set eyes upon his first steel mill, (in fact an iron foundry), that seemed to him almost blasphemous in size, in noise, origin, and purpose. All this, everything that lay within his view, *all* must be destroyed someday, destroyed for perhaps the ten thousandth time, (according to his readings), in order to atone for the mistakes of the first man. Ben groaned. And at the same time they ran down into the city itself, with its streets.

Never had he seen the like of this; almost the first thing to draw his notice was a nude mannequin beckoning from one of the windows. Flooded with anger, Ben said nothing. Nor had he ever viewed such crowds of people either, all passing wordlessly within inches of each other. He marked two men (grinning ones) who struck him as especially bad, while as for the *women*, they all appeared to be wearing their wealth upon their own persons. Here then, Ben divined, everything that was done, it was done because of the near-presence of others. Where were *Betty's* little brooches and bracelets? Never needed 'em. Moreover, there seemed to be a crisis going on here, with thousands in a panic to get where they wern't, as if where they were was so inferior to where they were going—Ben doubted it.

They parked, the speller getting out hastily and going his own way. The last he wanted was to throw away his Birmingham time in company with these, coarse types with "fun" in view. But first he must purchase gifts, and for his wife especially. And then too, he might buy something for Jasper as well. Fortunately, he had thought to bring a map; reading it, he collided into a tall man who bounced off and interfered with two others going in yet another direction.

"Hey! Fellow? You some kind of jerk or something?"

Ben leapt back. He was explaining, explaining calmly, but the man wouldn't stay to listen. Next he bumped shoulders with a distinguished-looking woman in jewelry and blued hair, who let out a moan. Ben could discover no other system for reading the map than to stand with his back against the building while at the same time trying earnestly not to think about his pressing need to urinate. Unfortunately, the map was of Atlanta. So far as he could make out, he had become glued to the north-northwestern corner of a quarter-section that, instead of cotton or corn, had been sown to tall buildings. Suddenly he stepped forth and headed away *in* the crowd, though not *of* it.

He had been planning for weeks about this gift, right up until the moment he saw a certain bolt of cloth in gorgeous display within a certain window; at once, he ran inside. That the clerk should happen to be all black, and better-dressed, and that she spoke a better grade of English that he did himself . . . He must remember to tell about this later on.

"Howdy," said Ben. "How much y'all asking for that speckled stuff?"

She laughed, the first time that ever he had been laughed at by a Negro in high heeled shoes.

"This *Sogdiane*?"

It even *sounded* speckled too. Taking off his glasses and reading it from two inches away, it seemed to Ben that he could detect in it all the smashing beauty of Persia, Turkey, and the rest, a "map" of colors complexer than Atlanta's.

"Yes, I take your meaning—Sog . . . Reckon I'll have eight dollars worth."

She was *not* awed by the amount—he had thought she would be. Quickly he counted it out, before the city, and the woman, before they could reconsider turning loose of so much beauty. Nor stopped till he was three blocks away.

His next search must be for his firstling, something brown, squat, and unmarriageable. Instead, it thwarted him to find that he had blundered into a most expensive district that specialized in diamonds and gauds of all sort, and further examples of those real-size "mannequins," this time including even a male—he assumed it was a male—holding a golf club in one hand. Ben came nearer. He had to admit it, it *was* in truth a near-nigh perfect copy of the authentic city type, with a face so fresh and clean and with nothing in it. What pleasures now, which sins and aberrations had not these people already tasted? And how many new ones still remained to be invented? Suddenly, Ben leapt high; behind him a car had come to a halt and was barking at a truck. The *other* cars, they were fussing at one another just like hens.

Of these objects and things, articles and rings, what should he acquire for Jasper and the others? For his second-eldest, it had to be hazel and/or green, marriageable, something she could *use*. What he bought therefore was a pen and two bottles of ink, both lovely, one green. For little Buford, who was not however so little anymore, Ben knew what the boy wanted. And knew further that what he wanted was not, and never had been, what he ought to have. Instead, the speller furrowed among the shoes and trousers, among pocket watches, (all of them far too grand for any pocket of Buford's), and then, coming back, among the trousers and shoes. Only at the very last moment did he settle upon something far more useful than any of these. As for Arsinoë, the sleepiest but yet also most marriageable of all his daughters, for her he bought a handbag in which she would immediately also find a pair of gloves.

Jasper's request was no longer in manufacture, wherefore Ben had to go deep, deep into a bad section of town before he could locate a pawnshop that, as it happened, was presided over by a mere boy of perhaps seventeen years who was himself also bad and who couldn't keep the sneer off his face. The store had all manner of things—tools and weapons, the ironmonger's art of fifty years ago and longer. Ben could have spent his whole time here, slowly turning over the artifacts and weighing them in his hand. For he had come to that point, already he had, of rue and regret for everything that was old, worn, crude, honorable, obsolete.

He came out, carrying his purchase in a little tin box well-secured with twine and tape. His intention was to find a place where he could take his lunch in private; instead, seeing a face that was quite unlike any that he had ever seen in his life, Ben fell in behind the person and followed for a short distance. It was a brisk gait, the man had. Ben marked it down, the stride, the lotion scent, and the briefcase too, committing it all to memory before veering off at last lest he burst out laughing and bring down more notice upon himself than he wanted, here in the big city midst.

The park, when he found it, he found it had a statue in it of one who during his life had gone about with a sword apparently and, apparently, had been near twice the size of the usual man. Here Ben squatted, testing the soil. It was loamy enough, and friable too; however, the whole vista had simply been put to grass. He did find a bench, but hardly had the time to spread his lunch before a woman came and settled not ten inches from the cornbread. Ben looked at her. This one had on rouge and lipstick and was continually glancing at her watch. To offer her anything from his lunch . . . He knew she wouldn't take it. And yet, the buttermilk struck him as particularly good this day, even if the beans were cold. He wolfed it all down with avidity—the woman had left—and lit his pipe. He had been missing from home only five hours, and yet already the place would be falling into decline. As for Buford taking any responsibility onto himself, Ben put no credence in it, not since the boy had bought a car of his own. Came now a second woman, seating herself on the bench opposite. Not only was she smoking, not only chewing gum, she also had her legs crossed in a certain way, wagging them in a manner that made Ben want to say something about it, and about other parts of her behavior as well.

Instead, he stood and marched off in a generally westwardly direction. A man came forward to meet him, a beggar with a beard and an accordion whom, at first, to judge by the twinkle in his eye, Ben judged to be a prophet or philosopher. Never would he (Ben) learn how to navigate within the city, having forever to dodge and backtrack, and slow down for the Birminghamians and their cars.

The moment having arrived, Ben entered the enormous auditorium and, moving on tiptoes, found a place between two other postmen representing counties far distant from his own. They shook. It was the dignity of it, the ambience, the quality of the people all sitting in absolute silence, many of whom, it seemed to Ben, looked just like himself. Some, yes, were drunk, but even these were quickly sobering up again, owing to the solemnity of the place. Someone coughed politely, a noise that was immediately followed up by the colors being brought in. There were now five men seated on stage, one of them so serious and worried-looking, the weight of the world on him . . . But it was the other, a thirty-year veteran, (as Ben learned later), who had the preponderance of the medals and wore the most brilliant sash. Ben could well imagine the postman *this* one had been. Compared to that, Ben had thrown his own life away and wasted it completely—such were his thoughts when the thirty-year man stood and began to speak.

Night did come, and yet Ben was still in the city. That he had lost contact with his colleagues, that they had gone back without him . . . There was nothing could be done about that now. More surprising was the number of pedestrians who were still up and abroad, despite that it was almost time to be in bed. And then too: neon. He had never seen some of these colors, fuzzy ones that gave off a hum. Once indeed he actually went up and put his finger on a certain one.

He trod on for a good two miles, walking like a farmer. His third surprise was of the silhouettes to be seen in the upper windows, people who ought to be in bed. (The absence of crickets comprised his fourth surprise.) Already he had passed one motion picture film theater, never in his wildest thoughts imagining that he might actually go inside such a place, not until he passed a second one and found the ticket-seller looking out so hopefully from her cage of glass, and so sweetly . . . Truth was, he needed to become more acquainted with film pictures, if only to learn whether it was something he should forbid to his children. He stopped, came back, fronted the woman. He was wearing his medal, conferred on him two hours ago, knowing that she could hardly fail to see it. "Howdy," he said. Someone, however, was crowding him from behind, a mere youth who, to his thinking, ought to have been home long before this.

His fifth surprise related to the theater itself: its general splendidness, its reverential silence, and the dense,

dense carpet that inspired him to take off his boots before going down into the aisle itself. No lack of seating
facilities—he chose a place that was as far away as possible from as many people as he could. Five minutes went
by. He found that he was staring up at a vast red curtain,
(velvet, it looked), on which, however, he could not for
the life of him see any film pictures whatsoever. He was
disappointed; reluctantly, he made ready to leave, and
would have done so but for that new person, his seventh
surprise, who had taken up at the end of the row and was
blocking off all egress. A boy walked by, his uniform
more striking than Benjamin's, a flashlight in one hand.

He waited ten minutes more before taking out the
slaw, the beans, and the last of the chicken gizzards. It
was true that Betty had wanted to come to Birmingham;
it explained why he had been given gizzards only, and
none of the white meat that he had come to expect from
her hand. All the same, this was far the most apt spot for
eating that he had so far found anywhere in the whole
city. He still did need to urinate however; indeed, he
needed it more than before. It was when he was lighting
up his pipe that, suddenly, the curtains opened with
great aplomb, revealing a huge gleaming screen that was
hard upon the eyes.

His eighth surprise—the enormousness of these ac-
tors, a race of giants; his thoughts flew back to that statue in the park. And though they conversed in the accents
of the North, still he was able to hear most of what they
were saying. He came slowly to realize that this particular motion picture film presentation had a bad man in it,
and out-and-out murderer, also a woman who, while no
doubt very beautiful, was continually drinking drinks
and smoking as well. But mostly, it was the underlying
philosophy that made Ben mad. He gave it half an hour
and then suddenly got up, pushed past the man at the
end, (who yelped), and then turned and came back for

Buford's gift.

It was bright night outside, but also very late. It mortified him to see himself reflected in a shop window, a fifty-five-year-old journeyman, somewhat smaller than he had believed, and with a moustache that looked as if it had been picked up off the street and attached, like his glasses, by a string that ran around his head. He had to say this too—the medal was also somewhat smaller than he had hoped. He could feel his old unbidden melancholy coming back; it joined with the never-ending grief in his kidneys, Abner's work.

It was nearly midnight when he ran into the statue again—it came to him that he might never break out of this town and city. Or, having coming out, that he might not have the fifty miles in him for getting back home again. It surprised him, his tenth such surprise, how that by night the buildings looked to have been built of water, and behind them, a green moon rising. He was in habit of thinking of himself as the equal of any city man, but when he saw *three* of them huddled under a lamp and looking back at him in a certain way . . . He ducked into an all-night cafe and came out on the other side.

A car came past, almost stopping for him—Ben smiled—before changing its mind at the last second. It was not now a green moon, but mustardly, ants swarming over it. He moved through a Negro neighborhood in which a small boy in a yellow raincoat was riding on his bicycle at two o'clock in the morning. Came next a gas station, the attendant quite asleep.

He believed that he was back into rural parts; instead, one mile further, he found himself among steel mills with myriads of laborers inside scampering back and forth amongst the yelling and the gleeds. Here, looking

out over the mills that in some measure compensated for
the absence of seas about Birmingham, Ben took a seat.
He was tired, tired to death, almost falling off to sleep
with a spoonful of beans halfway to his mouth. Remark-
ably, this was the moment the sun chose to poke up ex-
perimentally, to hesitate and blush—was he the *only* one
to notice it?—and then to drop back down again. It was
his fourteenth surprise.

He slept for twenty minutes. Or was it for a full day,
all around the clock, and *then* the twenty? In any case, he
was stronger now. On one side he had the city, (getting
brighter), and on the other, (getting dim), the county. He
must put on haste therefore, lest he run past his home in
the dark.

He straggled on until the sun came up in truth behind
those same tremulous buildings and lodged there. He
had brought no breakfast; fortunately, that was when a
good man came along, slowed, and opened his car. He
was good; Benjamin was not required to talk nor made to
tell anything about it. They drove the final 37 miles in
silence, covering the distance far more efficaciously that
Ben could have done by strolling. His heart was pound-
ing as they flew past Mitchell's place, past the field, and
then to the home that was his own, and his own people
crowding at the windows. But not for him. In awe and in
silence, they crowded for Jasper, Jasper always on the
lookout for airplanes, (or, as he believed, air*ships* with
sails), *he* it was that had expired at last and was lying in
the yard curled into a ball.

Thirty

And then one day he woke to find that he had grand-children, (three, not two), and now was in his most advanced fifties, (and no longer just twenty).

He wandered into the fields. Behind him, his entire work was on display, a life on the farm, and buildings he had builded for himself. Yes, he had to suppose that all this would fall into ruin someday, certainly it would, and that it would happen on that date when farms, (farms as a category of things), were no longer much needed. He had to hope that his own descendants at least would look back upon it kindly, or even with esteem, and not speak of him condescendingly, (remembering how he had wasted his life), in generations to come.

He was in the hen house peeping out through the slats when he saw a car coming down the lane and throwing up billows of red dust that wafted, not toward his own, (and Ben was grateful for this), but toward Mitchell's place. He knew, of course, what it was—how that one or another of his offspring would be bringing out one or another of *his*, or *her*, offsprings in order to humor the old man. Therefore Ben ran outside and, getting down painfully, hid himself in a furrow. They loved it, the old man hiding himself each time they came; indeed, he could hardly keep from laughing himself. Two crows flew over, neither of them greatly surprised to find him at his stunts.

It was the girl, Arsinoë's youngest, who came running. She jumped up and down, charmed, delighted, and thrilled to find an old man hiding in a furrow.

"I see you! I *see* you! I do!"

"Aw, shuckings!" He rose painfully. The mother, Ben's daughter, (she *used* to be a daughter), had gone inside. Now came little Leland Pefley, the most serious and glum of all his descendants. "Howdy, boy."

"Howdy."

"Looks to me like you need some *honey*. Want some? It's knowledge-producing."

The boy looked up at him with interest. "Knowledge?"

"Shore!"

They stood back fearfully while the old man strolled to his hive, opened it—he appeared to be oblivious to the bites—and then brought back two good-sized chunks of comb dripping with the sweetest of substances.

"Eat it! That's right. The wax too—that's where the wisdom is. Why, I can see your whole future, boy."

"You can?"

"Shore! But I can't tell you what it is."

"How come?"

"How come? Why, that wouldn't be right. No, you got to find out for yourself. Now! You want to go to the barn, talk to Cleo?"

They went. It was dim, the animals not speaking to each other at this time. The speller led them up straightway to the cow and pointed to the reflection in her eye.

"See? You can see just what she's thinking about."

"About me?"

"Yes, she was a fine woman, in her time. But now she's got to stay a cow for a few more years. She ain't allowed to *say* nothing, you understand."

They came nearer. It *was* a melancholy cow, burdened by memory. Arsinoë II was looking on sadly.

"Grandfather?"

"Yes?"

"Tell again how you used to hoodwink Cletus."

"He was a largish man . . ."

"Grandfather!"

"What!"

"Tell about *Barlaam*."

"Barlaam! Your mother loved that hog."

"Grandfather!"

Etc., etc.

That night, he hid again, even in the same furrow. He saw the girl come out with the lantern and dog and go off searching among the buildings. Himself, in his soiled clothes, he could not be distinguished from the earth. Soon enough, his mind began to wander.

He was looking into the region of "The Mule," very brilliant on this night. The last time he had looked, its component stars had been so confused with those of "The Lizard" that he had never thought to find them discrete again, one from the other. And then his attention was caught by the moonbright, and frightened fireflies chased in and out of its beams by a darkling batflight on the wing; its noise worried him. Now suddenly the dog ran past, more interested in other things than Ben.

Ben had to laugh. He had gotten his starbright, to be sure, but now it was late, he himself tired, and a long, long time before daybreak, or "dawn," so-called, dawn, light, the guarantee of clouds in unprecedented shapes, and a strange new day for clarity, for seeing, and for strangeness itself.

Thirty-one

Time was winding down, he could feel it. These days, old as he was, the crows winked as they passed over, fearing him no longer. Things had *not* worked out as he had planned, he was *not* less unadvanced than when he had started out. And then too, these latter days, he sometimes heard rumors of disquiet coming from Europe, Asia, and/or Latin America.

Nevertheless, he now took up his hoe and went forward with it. His wife, the woman, her whom he had married, these days her bonnet had turned white in token of her own white hair. Ben started to follow, but then gave over when he saw that she was traveling too fast. Where was she going, what fruits and diamonds did she seek, and what would she bring back in her enormous basket? He knew this, that in these days she would eat of naught save only occasional wheat groats poached in milk. Still, he had to laugh; hardly had she entered the trees before once more bursting out, even as she had burst out every day of the year for the past forty such years, singing *The Old Grey Goose is Dead* in her mournful voice.

Ben labored on. He had numerous difficulties, and one difficulty especially—it resided in his liver—and so why therefore was he smiling? All his brothers were dead, save one only, his second-favorite who, however, had lately been constrained to the inebriate asylum. Other problems also oppressed him, especially his second-favorite grandson. Apparently the poor boy had had a sorry experience with love, and now was holding out alone in earthquake-ravaged Helice. Ben halted, took out his pad and pencil, and noted it down to visit him someday.

He went on smiling however. Give him six months and he'd be retired and on pension, his *government-funded* pension, very highly dependable. Yes, it had been a long time. And now, once retired, he could begin to repair his own educational unadvancement, using for that purpose some of his own forty books, or somewhat more.

The sun was high, suffering for oxygen; it seethed about the edges. Looking into it, Ben said: "I wanted to use me up and throw me away." Then: "What else *could* I do?" His buildings were in good repair, he had sixteen boxes of bees. And yet . . . And yet . . . He knew it as clearly as if he had foreseen it in a dream—how that all this, land, bees, woman and hens, how that in times to come it would be looked upon as having been charming at best, or even merely picturesque.

He had wasted his life, he had had to admit it to himself these last few years. Let him retire and *then* let him find out what he can do. Build him a tower first, a "star steeple," (he called it), *that* was his first and most pressing project. He had been saving up the bricks and glue.

But would the world endure so long? For of all his problems, none worried him so much as these increasing disturbances in the sky, this misalignment of objects that harkened him back to that time along the Edge when in great heedlessness he used to . . . Suddenly, Ben stopped, gasped, and then, shielding his eyes, looked more closely into the north-northeastern corner where, to his absolute amazement, he now saw what looked to be an entire nation on the march, which is to say two Negroes, an albino, three Negroids together with yet another who appeared only slightly Negroloidalisticistic, all of them migrating with mules and luggage across his land. And if they *faced* into the sun, yet their *eyes* were upon the seeming promise of Georgia's western hills.

Thirty-two

It was with but eight days before retirement that he turned aside from his route and went two miles out of his way. The day was clear, and the clouds that might otherwise have "peopled" the sky, they had all gone elsewhere. Here, far from the highway, the Negroes saluted him courteously, while as for those who had borrowed from him, *they* saluted twice in lieu of paying back.

Today, Ben did not turn off onto that knoll, (becoming known as "Postman's Roost"), where the view was at its best. Instead, he went half a mile further, into an abandoned section, and then down into the extinct farm-stead where Belinda used to live.

It was overgrown, there where the house had stood; still, he was able to go and stand in the site where they been sitting on that day. He could have found things possibly, had he wanted to dig for them—a comb, bits of red ribbon. His attention focused on the windmill, its one remaining blade still turning slowly.

He went to the barn, entered, and stood for a time. There was no roof, of course, not after so many years and a history of high winds, and so Ben found himself looking skyward with that same puzzled expression that he had been wearing since his first visit to this place.

He came out, whereupon, suddenly, the wind took his hat and blew it far away. He was in no condition to chase it. Instead, he wandered on farther, down to the creek, where he stood listening. What thoughts had he, which memories, how long did he stay? In fact, he was grinning again. His wife must never hear of this, how he had come so far out of his way, and with so much mail still needing to be delivered. His hat was far away; nevertheless, Ben now checked up and down the road in both directions, doing it carefully before he dared to get down, making himself invisible, and so to sleep a while in the summer grass.

Thirty-three

He got *all* his answers in August. He was out in the field "sun-gazing," (as he called it), when his heart, worn down by now to an amazing thinness, exploded. He fell. Fortunately, Betty was out in the yard. Unfortunately, she didn't see him.

It was his sixty-fourth surprise—to find that he had ascended and was floating face-down over a map, not of 1936 indeed, but of Alabama in 1874. Interestingly, he was able to discern many of the farms and even some of the same unpaved roads that he seemed to remember. Now, every feature was well-captioned with mile-high lettering that ran across the rather complicated terrain. Never looking *upward*, his wife failed to note him.

But what towns did he see, which streams, whose houses? Certainly he could feel the stars that had been pinned to him, nine in number; they formed an outline very like his own former self. To his surprise, Belinda lived now in Methana County; he could see the place behind her ear. However, it was tiring at this altitude and soon he flew down to a somewhat lower level, there to rest. It was all a dream.

In fact, he dreamt that he was in his father's house, that he was new, the earth outside smoldering, and his brothers calling, calling him to come and play.

About the Author

Tito Perdue was born in 1938 in Chile, the son of an electrical engineer from Alabama. The family returned to Alabama in 1941, where Tito graduated from the Indian Springs School, a private academy near Birmingham, in 1956. He then attended Antioch College in Ohio for a year, before being expelled for cohabitating with a female student, Judy Clark. In 1957, they were married, and remain so today. He graduated from the University of Texas in 1961, and spent some time working in New York City, an experience which garnered him his life-long hatred of urban life. After holding positions at various university libraries, Tito has devoted himself full-time to writing since 1983.

His first novel, 1991's *Lee*, received favorable reviews in *The New York Times, The Los Angeles Reader,* and *The New England Review of Books.* In addition to the present volume, his novels include *The New Austerities* (1994), *The Sweet-Scented Manuscript* (2004), *Fields of Asphodel* (2007), *The Node* (2011), *Morning Crafts* (2013), *Reuben* (2014), the *William's House* quartet (2016), *Cynosura* (2017), *Philip* (2017), *Though We Be Dead, Yet Our Day Will Come* (2018), *The Bent Pyramid* (2018), *The Philatelist* (2018), *The Smut Book* (2018), *The Gizmo* (2019), *Love Song of the Australopiths* (2020), *Materials for All Future Historians* (2020), *Journey to a Location* (2021), and *Vade Mecum* (2021)—which have been praised in *Chronicles: A Magazine of American Culture, The Quarterly Review, The Occidental Observer,* and at *Counter-Currents.*

In 2015, he received the H. P. Lovecraft Prize for Literature.

.